The Blooming of
the Flame Tree

The Blooming of the Flame Tree

Roberta Lunsford Kehle

CROSSWAY BOOKS • WESTCHESTER, ILLINOIS
A DIVISION OF GOOD NEWS PUBLISHERS

F-46

The Blooming of the Flame Tree.
Copyright ©1983 by Roberta Lunsford Kehle.
A Crossway Youth Book,
published by Good News Publishers,
Westchester, Illinois 60153.

Cover illustration by Gloria Phillips
Cover design by Curtis Lundgren

First printing, 1983
Second printing, 1983
Printed in the United States of America

Library of Congress Catalog Card Number 82-83635

ISBN 0-89107-275-6

1

The wild eyes of the water buffalo focused on Tran. Its nostrils flared with excited snorts, and Tran held his kite closer to his side, his muscles tensed.

The driver of the cart behind the buffalo lashed out with his whip as he tried to turn the horned animal stubbornly standing crosswise to the early morning traffic. "Go, you stupid beast!" he shouted. But the creature, frightened by honking car horns and swerving bicyclists, charged suddenly toward the corner where Tran stood, causing a group of women to scream and flail their market baskets. Tran leaped to one side.

At last the old man persuaded the excited animal to turn, and with a lurch the cart continued to bump its way along the rutted street. The women, after chirping insults at the pair, crossed the street, chatting under their orange paper parasols.

A boy near Tran exclaimed angrily, "It is 1976—water buffaloes have no place in the cities of Laos! They belong in the rice paddies!"

Tran stretched his legs into a run and headed for the grassy hill near town that for generations had been the scene of kite contests. His thoughts raced with him. That old cart driver, from a country village, was used to doing things the same way as always. He probably couldn't read or write. How wonderful it would be when teachers and schools were in all parts of Laos.

Halfway up the slope, Tran slowed and paused to catch

his breath while he gazed down at his town's yellow stucco buildings with their weathered red roofs, standing as a reminder of the old French rule. Why do people always want to control other people? He kicked at the ground with his sandal, and thought of the recent stories of Vietnamese troops invading the mountain Hmong villages where his mother was reared. They had wasted no time after the Americans had quit fighting them and had left Southeast Asia.

Why can't the Communists leave us in peace? He kicked at the ground again, then hurried on to have some flying time before school started.

When he reached the top of the hill, the sky was already filled with flashes of color. Tran thought this must be his favorite sight—red, blue, yellow and purple shapes, swooping, dodging and darting. The long colorful tails on the kites fluttered in the breeze like butterfly wings.

He liked this part better than fighting with the kites, but he was in the competition and should do his best. His own star-shaped frame shuddered as it slipped into an air current, then sailed confidently into the midst of the others.

"Okay, Blue Star," he whispered, "let's go!" Tran flicked his wrist, and the kite caught the string of a red fish. He sawed with all his might and smiled as his line cut the other one.

The owner of the red fish picked up his kite from the ground and walked over to Tran. "My kite now belongs to you."

"No, Sy," said Tran. "You keep it. After all the work you did on it, it would be a shame to lose it."

"Tran, you never do as the other boys. Why don't you keep the kites you have won?"

Tran shrugged. "I do not like to make anyone feel sad. And I know how sad I would feel if the Blue Star were taken from me."

"No chance of that!" Sy laughed. "You are the best kite fighter around. After school, maybe you could give me some help in my maneuvers."

Tran and Sy raced down the hill to the government intermediate school building. Soon other twelve-year-old boys, all wearing the same kind of blue trousers and white shirts, assembled in the classroom. They stood by their desks, pressed their hands together, and gave the teacher a slight bow of greeting.

In a few minutes, Tran was busy working a mathematic problem. He enjoyed mathematics. It was like a game to see if he could do it right, and it gave him a satisfied feeling when he did.

Flies buzzing and the noise of the big wooden fan on the ceiling were the only sounds in the room. He finished the question and looked around.

Some class members worked hard on the problem, their foreheads wrinkled in thought. Others looked out the open window, maybe thinking more about kite flying than mathematics. But just as the daydreamers were about to receive the customary rap on the hand, the headmaster hurried into the room. He beckoned the teacher aside, whispered something in his ear, and quickly left.

The teacher tapped his desk with a ruler and cleared his throat. "Gentlemen, we have expected it for some time; but now invasion from the Vietnamese is indeed close."

Tran stared in disbelief as the teacher continued. "There will be no school until further notice. I advise you all to go to your homes." He stopped and swallowed hard. "Never stop learning. Good-bye."

The boys bowed and silently filed out the door. Tran had a sick feeling in his stomach. He wondered if the others did too. Even though some, including his father, had expected Vietnam to invade the lowland towns, everyone hoped it wouldn't happen.

As Tran thought of his father, he had an overwhelming desire to get home. He broke into a run, dodging people on the street.

"Tran Savang! Wait!" Sy's voice, behind him, was becoming closer as he raced to catch up. "You left school so fast," he panted as he skidded to a stop beside Tran. "You were going to give me some help, remember?" He cupped one hand and made climbing and swooping motions in the air.

"Kites? Sy, didn't you hear what the teacher said?"

"Oh, that." Sy laughed. "My father says the Vietnamese government just wants to scare us. They won't send troops to invade our town. Why should they? Our government lets them use our country as a base for invading Cambodia. What else do they want? You'll see. We'll get a short holiday from school and then everything will be the way it was."

"But Father has been saying—" began Tran.

"Listen, my friend," said Sy, "your father may be the headmaster of the secondary school and very smart, but my father's connections in his import store let him know what is going on around Southeast Asia. He won't leave his store. You worry too much. Let's meet for a Coca-Cola tomorrow and talk about kites." He waved and disappeared in the direction of his father's shop.

Tran gazed after him. Father had said that if the Communists came, the teachers and educated people would be the first to be killed. But that didn't make sense. Perhaps the teacher was wrong anyway—the Communists wouldn't harm them. Maybe it would be as Sy said, and there would be more contests with his Blue Star and then a bicycle to look forward to. He had saved his money, earned by doing errands for shop owners, and now had 7,000 kip, nearly enough for the bicycle he wanted. That thought made him feel better.

4

He sprinted across the street. The morning was already hot, for the monsoon winds that brought refreshing summer rain were late this year. After a while he slowed his pace and examined the flame trees planted at intervals along the street. They always bloomed just before the monsoons came, and they were showing color! In a few days each would be a cloud of reddish orange, transforming the shabby buildings and hiding the bold new ones that Tran didn't think looked very elegant. Perhaps the one in front of his house was also ready to bloom!

Tran squinted toward the highest hill outside of town. Heat waves made the Buddhist temple at the top look eerie and dreamlike. The gold serpents on its black tiled roof looked as though they were floating—floating on a river, searching for prey. Tran felt a sudden feeling of foreboding and averted his eyes.

When he entered the house, his mother was setting out her cherished black and gold teacups. The look on her face brought back the sick feeling in his stomach. It was the same look she had worn when they thought his little sister Sun would die from an illness. Friends came and cried then. But Mother was from the brave Hmong tribe of the mountains of Laos, and they do not cry. She had prayed, pulled herself to every inch of her stature, and said, "Now, what will be, will be." And there had been that look, serious and set and calm, all at once.

Sun got better and Tran hadn't seen that look until now.

"Your father wishes you in the other room." Mother kept her dark eyes on the tea and didn't seem to notice a wayward strand of hair that had escaped from her bun.

Father was home too? Tran allowed the ceiling fan to blow on his hot face. For an instant he let himself imagine

5

that this was an ordinary day. The house, with its slatted walls between each room, was cool and airy, and he would do his lessons at the teakwood desk his father had built. Mother would prepare fish curry for dinner, and he could almost smell the spiciness.

The daydream ended when Mother moved toward him with the tray. Tran took a deep breath. *I should be more like Mother and my Hmong ancestors*, he thought—*brave, no matter what happens*.

As he walked in to meet his father, the sick feeling left, but a hard lump remained. His baby sister, three-year-old Paw, played in the corner of the room. "Twan," she cried, and ran to him with arms upstretched.

Father and the pastor of their Christian mission church sat together, deep in conversation. Mother set the tray on the low table and picked up Paw. "There is a sesame cake for you, Daughter."

Her black sandals made scrunching sounds as she took Paw away, and her expression had not changed. She neither smiled nor frowned.

"Son," said Father, "Pastor Oh told me distressing news, and though you are twelve you are old enough to discuss it with us."

Tran gave a slight bow to his father and the pastor and sat down. He couldn't remember when Pastor Oh had not been their friend. Father once told him that the pastor had suffered awful things at the hands of the Vietnamese Communists because not only was he a Christian (they feared Christians), but he was of Chinese descent (which they hated). He had escaped to Laos, and it was from him that Father learned about Christianity. Now Father was a Christian instead of a Buddhist, and Mother, who had once worshiped many different spirits at the same time, was also a Christian.

6

Usually when the pastor saw him he would say how tall Tran was getting and tease Father about having to look up to his son. But this time he only looked at Tran with sad eyes, and suddenly Tran noticed that the pastor's hair was white and that his face was wrinkled. *He looks old*, Tran thought.

Pastor Oh spoke wearily. "I received news that Vietnamese soldiers, with the help of their friends in our government, have invaded a town only fifty miles from here. The people were driven from their homes and forced to walk around the city without food or rest. All teachers, ministers and Buddhist priests were imprisoned."

The lump in Tran's stomach got bigger and tighter, and his knees felt weak. Sy was wrong! He looked at his father. Tran was always pleased when people said he looked just like him. His father had the lowland Laotian light-brown skin and unslanted dark eyes, and his black hair waved slightly. He usually had a smile, but now he too looked tired and old.

Father poured tea in the cups. "We cannot wait any longer. When they come, our family will certainly be separated. We must leave."

"When?" Mother had slipped back into the room.

"Tonight," came the quiet answer. "Pastor Oh thinks that if we can get across the miles of bushland between here and the Mekong River, we might be able to reach safety."

Tran wondered if he was having a bad dream. But he could feel the hotness of the tea in his throat. That wasn't possible in a dream, was it?

Mother stood up. "What should we take?"

"Very little," said Pastor Oh. "You have many miles to travel, and you will need your strength to carry food and other necessities. Also, a small boat won't have much room."

"Will you go with us?" Tran finally found his voice.

"No, son," said the kindly pastor. "I must stay and help others escape, and be of comfort to those who can't."

Tran felt hot tears sting his eyes. They would never see him again!

Pastor Oh stood and put one hand on Tran's shoulder and one on his father's. Mother joined them to make a circle. He prayed for their safety, and then he and Father clasped each other.

"If we don't see each other again here on earth, we will in Heaven. Go with God." With that, he left.

Father had tears in his eyes, but Mother's expression didn't change. She said in a matter of fact voice, "We had better begin."

Father wiped his eyes and straightened his shoulders. "We need to pack food that will not spoil, bedding for sleeping on the ground, and ointment for an injury," he said. "Set aside food for a good meal before we leave. Tran, help me with the bedding. Sun can help Mother. Where *is* Sun?"

"*Bon jour*." A smiling round face with front teeth that stuck out a little peeped in from the other room. "We were excused early from school, but I had to help a girl in a higher level with her French verbs. She needed to study while school is closed, and the teacher said that even if I am only ten, my French is better than some in the secondary school."

Tran smiled at his younger sister. "That is right. You are better than I in French."

"But you are better in mathematics," she offered.

"Children! Time is important." Father picked up Sun as though she were Paw's age. "We have to pack a few things and leave our home quickly, before soldiers come. Do you understand?"

Sun wrinkled her nose. "Do we have to leave forever? My friend and I are giving a shadow puppet play next week."

"We don't know, Small Princess," said Father softly. "But what is important is that we are together and safe, no matter where we are. Now you must do as your mother says."

"*Oui.* It will be an adventure. What will we do, Mother?"

Father didn't tell her about the invasion or where we are going, thought Tran. He felt grown-up and as old as Father.

Mother prepared a dinner of rice and pieces of barbecued pork, eggplant, and red and green chilis on a skewer. She also cut up a large golden pineapple from their garden.

Tran wasn't hungry, but he tried to force himself to eat because Father said they needed strength for the journey.

He scooped up a wad of sticky rice from the basket and squeezed it into a roll. "Why are educated people the ones Communists hate most? I don't understand."

Father dipped his rice roll into the hot sauce and took a bite before answering. "Because, Son, Communists want to control people's minds, and the only way they can do that is if the people don't know about or can't read about other kinds of governments."

"I see," Tran said slowly. "And ministers, priests and teachers would tell others about Communism." He thought a moment. "I guess we need money to get to another country." Tran excused himself and went to his sleeping room. He rummaged around in his wooden chest until he found a cloth bag tied at the top.

"Here, Father," he said, returning to the table. "Seven thousand kip. It isn't much, but it might help."

"Oh, I *hate* the Communists!" cried Sun. "That was Tran's bicycle money!"

Father's hand reached out and covered Sun's. "Small Princess, don't hate people. You may hate the things they do, but if you hate them you are as guilty as they." He turned to Tran. "Thank you, Son. It will indeed help. And I promise you that if it is at all in my power, one day I shall buy you the finest bicycle that is made."

Tran thought Mother's expression changed a little as she hugged him and said, "Thank you, Son."

"It is nearly time to go," said Father. "We must do as much traveling in the dark as possible, so the soldiers won't see us. Tran and I will fill water bottles."

"And I will put the meal things in order," said Mother. "Not even for Communists will I leave an untidy house! Besides," she said softly, "I wish to touch my beautiful dishes once more." She lovingly fingered the black and gold tea set.

When the tasks were finished, and they were together, ready to start, Tran excused himself. There were two more things he must do.

First, he went to the cupboard where Mother kept her dishes and took down a small black and gold flowered plate. He wrapped it around and around with one of his shirts and carefully put it in the center of his small backpack. Then he went to his sleeping room and picked up his kite.

"Blue Star," he whispered, "not for anything would I want unfriendly hands to touch you. It is better that you are free."

He took the kite outside where a light breeze was blowing and in a few seconds had it launched into the night sky. Then he took out his knife and, hesitating for an instant, cut the string. He could hear the kite flutter as it floated away.

Scalding tears blurred his eyes and his throat ached, but he swallowed hard, turned around, and went into the house to join the family.

Mother had taken a length of soft cloth and was tying it over the mouth of the sleeping Paw.

"What are you doing, Mother?" asked Sun as she yawned and rubbed her eyes.

"This is in case Paw should wake up and make noise at a time when we have to be very quiet."

10

Father hoisted Paw onto his back and put another pack around his neck. Mother, Sun and Tran each carried a small pack. They went out the door and softly closed it behind them. No one looked back, but Tran, looking into the black sky, imagined he saw the outline of his kite over the city.

Good-bye, Blue Star. He mouthed the words silently. *I don't know what will happen to us, but I am thankful you are free.*

2

The moon was an orange ball, low on the horizon, and by its light Tran saw shadowy figures hurrying along the street.

Word has spread about the invasion, he thought. Another thought occurred to him. Sy! Would he and his family escape? He wished he could find out.

The silver motor-bicycle Father rode to school each day stood by the porch. He motioned Tran to push it.

"This will be of no use to us," muttered Tran as he rolled it behind his parents. "Why does he wish to take it?"

"What did you say?" Sun whispered at his side.

"Nothing important." Tran bumped his knee against the bicycle's pedal. "Are you sleepy, Sun?"

"I was—in the house, but not now. I'm too excited."

"Why are you whispering?" Tran asked, though he found himself doing the same thing. "The Communists aren't around us yet."

"It seems more adventurous. Besides, I must make myself get used to doing so. I might blurt out something when we have to be quiet. I talk a lot, you know."

Tran smiled. He knew, but he had never minded the bubbles of joy his sister bestowed every place she went.

"Tran," Sun's whisper came again. "I did something selfish and bad, and I am worried that I will get in trouble."

Tran sighed. They didn't need another problem right now. "What did you do?"

"I brought—"

But just then the uneven paving on the road caused the

motor-bicycle to lurch. "Aahh!" Tran cried. He gripped the handlebars more firmly. "I should also practice *my* whispering."

Families carrying belongings thronged the streets. Some pushed motor-bicycles as he did. Why?

Sun seemed to forget her confession and tapped Tran's shoulder. "Look."

A lamp inside a nearby house illuminated a family packing a Buddhist shrine.

"They must be taking it with them," Sun whispered. "But that statue will be heavy to carry."

"The need for God is in each of us," Tran answered. "If our family were still Buddhists instead of Christians, we too would take along our image."

"Well, I did," giggled Sun. "Except mine is inside me where it isn't a burden to carry, and saves room besides!"

The moon inched its way further in the sky and turned from orange to gold. They left the city behind and for some time trekked along a country road thick with dust and stones that spit from the motor-bicycle's tires onto Tran's legs. His back ached from bending over the bicycle, and his shoulder and neck muscles were tight from trying to keep his pack centered. It was with great relief that he finally heard Father say, "It's time we rest awhile by the side of the road."

They had been walking in single file, quiet Sun holding on to the back of the motor-bicycle with one hand. Tran guessed she had her eyes closed and was letting the bike guide her.

An oxcart rumbled by. Then a family like theirs passed them, the mother and father each carrying a child. Would everyone make it to safety, Tran wondered.

Father swung Paw gently down to the grass by the road.

She made soft noises of protest at having her sleep interrupted, and then fell again into slumber. Everyone had a long drink of cool water, and Mother handed out sesame cakes. They had never tasted so good to Tran, and he ate hungrily with one hand, while his other massaged his neck.

Sun took two bites of a cake, then fell asleep, propped against her mother.

Father spoke in a low voice. "I purposely didn't mention full details of our journey, because the last hours in our home should have been ones of peace, not turmoil from fear."

He took another swallow of water. "I had first thought we would cross the Mekong River to Thailand, which is free."

Tran's tired body sat up straighter. That wouldn't be far to travel. The river, which formed the boundary between the countries, was near.

"But," went on Father, "I understand the border has closed. And what we must do demands greater courage, but I believe we can succeed. We must," he said so softly Tran could hardly hear his words.

Father's voice grew stronger. "We'll travel to the river, below the rapids, and barter with someone for a boat to take us down the river and into the sea."

"But, Father!" The lump was back in Tran's stomach. "That will take us through Cambodia and part of Vietnam. We'll never make it past the Communists!"

Father came over and put a hand on Tran's shoulder. "If we get a good boat, my son, we have a chance. That's why we are bringing the motor-bicycle. Everything of value will have to be traded for passage."

Suddenly the quiet air was split by the sound of gunfire. Mother screamed, while Tran, his heart beating, jumped up

14

and tried to see into the blackness. "That's coming from our town!"

"The troops made faster time than we thought. Hurry, everyone!" shouted Father. "There is no time to spare!" He hitched his pack over his chest. "We must walk until dawn, then find a place to hide during the daylight hours. I'll carry Sun for awhile, and Mother Paw. Tran, can you manage the motor-bicycle again?"

"Yes, sir." Tran forced his tired back and shoulders to attention. Now that he knew this bicycle might mean safety for them, he could push it forever!

The moon had slipped over the other side of the sky to make room for an approaching sun. The straps from Tran's pack cut into his shoulders, and dust from the road filled his nose and made him cough. He thought of Pastor Oh's description of how the people in the neighboring town had been treated, and he worried about Sy and his family. Had they escaped? And was Mother thinking about strange people in her house, perhaps breaking her dishes? He remembered her telling the story of her father, a wealthy Hmong chief, sending her to school in lowland Laos, and how she met Father there. When they decided to marry, his family wouldn't speak to him for marrying a Hmong, and her family wouldn't speak to her for marrying a lowlander.

The only friend Mother and Father had then, the headmaster of the school, gave them a china set as a wedding gift, and Mother had treasured it ever since. Tran was glad he brought the plate.

Finally Father stopped and motioned the family to follow him into the dense growth of vegetation along the road.

It was still dark in the forest, although faint streaks of

15

pink had replaced the stars behind them. Vines laced themselves between the bamboo and palm trees, and it wasn't easy to push the motor-bicycle through them. Tran felt as though he were in a gigantic cobweb, but the thought of rest made him push harder into the thick underbrush.

Sun, who catnapped for awhile on Father's back, was again trudging behind Tran, and fought her way through with both hands. Even Paw, awakening several miles before to find a cloth around her mouth, flailed her arms from her perch on Mother's back.

"Mmmph," she said as she ducked her head against Mother's neck.

It was growing lighter now, and they could pick their way more easily. Soon they came to the dry, cracked bed of a stream. When the rains came, it would be filled with rushing water; but now they crossed it, and went into a small clearing between groves of thick bamboo. It made a hidden shelter for them, and Mother unrolled the sleeping mats on the ground.

Then she untied Paw's cloth, but put her hand over the little girl's mouth as a sign that she must be quiet.

Tran took a drink of water, lay down, and shut his eyes. It felt so good to stretch out flat. He wouldn't go to sleep, for he must help Father guard.

When he opened his eyes, he didn't know where he was. Hot fingers of sun touched his cheek. He looked at his surroundings. Paw was curled up on Mother's dusty black skirt. Sun slept on a mat, one leg jerking every few seconds. Then Tran remembered.

Father dozed in an upright position on his mat. *This moment will stay with me forever*, Tran thought. *The fact that we have all been asleep, not knowing who or what was around us, and yet we have been cared for and are safe.*

16

He got quietly to his feet, but the small movement brought Father's head up with a snap. He glanced at the rest of his sleeping family to make sure they were all right, then gave a nod and smile to Tran, who motioned he wished to go into the bamboo thicket.

The rays of sunshine that had touched Tran told him it was late in the day. He retraced the family's steps to the dry stream bed, where he stretched his arms and tried to exercise the stiffness from his joints. How he wished the stream had water so he could bathe his perspiring face.

His eyes scanned the sky. No clouds were in sight. Only a bird flying in the distance broke up the blurry blueness. The bird grew larger, and suddenly terror seized Tran. That was a helicopter! Nearer it came, just above the trees, racing along the path taken by the stream. His legs grew so weak they trembled, and he couldn't move.

3

Tran dove back into the thicket of trees, dropped to the ground, and held his breath. Had they seen him? He felt his heart beating wildly against his ribs as he lay motionless and listened to the oncoming drone of the giant metal bird.

In a few seconds there was a loud, fast, chopping sound, as the helicopter roared over the spot where he had stood a moment before.

He wished he could burrow farther into the ground, but he did not dare to move. He knew little about helicopters. Did they have some device that allowed the soldiers to see into the jungle?

Machine-gun fire suddenly ripped the air. They *had* seen him! His pounding heart seemed to stop beating, and he thought of his mother's face when she learned he had been killed. Would she cry?

The spine-chilling sound continued. *I should have been hit by now*, Tran thought. He slowly raised his head and through the treetops could see bright, white lights streaking over him into the jungle.

They look like the rockets we shoot at New Year's, he thought in wonderment. As fast as it began, the gunfire stopped and the rhythmic chopping turned back into a drone. Stillness surrounded him again.

While he considered what to do, a thought struck him. They had shot into the jungle! Mother and Father were back there! And Sun! And Paw!

Tears filled his eyes as he pushed through the trees. He

propelled himself blindly through the undergrowth. Vines and sharp bamboo reached out scratchy fingernails and mixed blood and tears on his face.

"Father!" he cried as he reached the clearing. He stopped in disbelief. The mats were still unrolled and the packs lying next to them, but his family was gone!

"Father." This time it was a soft, pathetic cry. He whirled at the rustle of branches. The bamboo stalks parted, and Father's familiar and comforting figure stepped out.

"Son! You're all right. God be thanked. Mother, bring out the girls!"

Everyone's arms went around everyone else. Even Paw danced up and down, grabbing legs.

"We thought you were killed!" Sun's cheeks were streaked with tears. "Tran! What happened to your face?"

"I thought you were too," said Tran. "And I was in a hurry to get back!"

Father said, "We didn't hear the helicopter until it was nearly overhead!"

"We had to leave everything and run for the trees," interrupted Sun.

"The tracer bullets went over our heads, so we knew we weren't the targets. We thought perhaps they got you in the first blast." Father's arms went around Tran again.

"Those white streaks. What were they?" asked Tran excitedly.

"The soldiers put phosphorus in some of the bullets to show where they are landing." Father sighed and shook his head. "They were aimed at someone else hiding in the jungle. I hope they didn't find their mark."

Mother cupped Tran's chin in her hand. "You need ointment on those bad scratches."

She poured a little water from a bottle and tenderly

bathed Tran's face. As she soothed on the cooling salve, he murmured, "It is said that the Hmongs are too tough to cry. I did them dishonor today, for I cried as I ran back."

Mother's fingers didn't miss a stroke, but she looked into his eyes. "For whom did you cry?"

Tran said nothing. He didn't know.

The points of sunlight that had managed to work their way through the dense foliage were now blocked. The clearing was dusky. Tran shivered. A short while ago he wished for coolness. Now he longed to feel a hot cup of tea between his palms. But they dared not build a fire.

Mother took packages from her pack. "I should have brought some kind of dishes for food."

Tran jumped up. "I know!" He took his knife from his pocket and cut five leaves from a wild banana tree that draped nearby. "Dishes for everyone," he said triumphantly.

Sun clapped her hands. "I used these for play dishes when I was small. I remember thinking my dish was taller than I!" She held one beside Paw. Paw looked up at the tip which towered over her head, then reached out her arms to wrap the leaf around her.

"No, Little Sister," Tran laughed. "It isn't good manners to wrap your dish around you!"

Mother put on each leaf a piece of barbecued pork from yesterday, a cold rice roll, and wedges of the juicy pineapple they had cut up last night.

Tran squatted by his place. He was starved. It had been a long time since their last meal.

Father said the blessing. He gave thanks for the food, thanks for their safety, and (ahead of time) thanks for their continued safety and direction.

Tran wished Father would hurry, especially when he

opened his eyes a crack and saw hordes of ants and other slithery insects crawling toward their food. When Father finished the prayer, Sun stifled a scream as she tried to brush a beady-eyed creature from her piece of meat.

But even repulsive pests wouldn't stop Tran from enjoying his meal. The only sound during the rest of the meal was made by hundreds of toads, unaware of enemy invasion, croaking their song to the night.

"May I have some water?" Tran asked when he was through.

"We must save the water. If you are thirsty, have some pineapple," Mother answered.

Sun took a wedge and noisily sucked out the juice before she ate the yellow meat. Tran didn't want any. The juice would be sticky, and it wouldn't be the same as cool water. Would there ever again be plenty of that?

It was so dark now, it was hard to see the family. Father took his large flashlight from his pack and, shielding it, turned it on so Mother could see to wrap the remaining food and tie the cloth around Paw's mouth.

Tran winced as he hitched his pack over his tender shoulders. He felt for the handlebars of the motor-bicycle.

Father switched off the torch, plunging them into blackness. "We will go back to the road through the forest ahead, not back to the stream bed. We'll go slowly because it will be difficult with only one light. We have to trust that the Communists haven't yet mined the road." He paused, and then his voice seemed harsh to Tran. "The helicopter won't be our greatest time of fear, my family. There will be worse moments ahead of us."

Sun began to cry. "I don't want to be frightened any more!"

"Nor do any of us, Small Princess." His voice softened.

"But if this were our greatest taste of fear, we wouldn't be worthy to stand beside such people as Pastor Oh, who suffered much to be free. Remember, you will be given courage at the time you need it. Not before, but *when* you need it."

He turned and started through the brush, with his family following. Tran thought the beam of light seemed very faraway. Would he lose sight of it?

He couldn't protect his face because he had to push the bicycle, and he almost cried aloud as branches whipped his raw skin. He heard Sun thrashing ahead of him.

The shaft of light from Father's torch served only to show what direction to take. It didn't show the rough stones or holes in the ground. They cropped up unexpectedly and made Tran fall more than once, the bicycle on top of him.

When would they get through this terrible place? Had the Communists already mined the road? And if they did reach the Mekong, what would happen to them?

I don't want to go on, he cried to himself. *Maybe it's better to go back and be under the Communists. They can't be so evil.*

He opened his mouth to call Father, but at that moment a hand from the dark clamped harshly over his mouth.

4

Something cold and hard rammed into Tran's back and shoved him roughly ahead. His throat muscles screamed in pain at the force of the jerk, and for an instant he couldn't breathe! The bicycle fell from his grasp, and with his head yanked back his face was defenseless against the stinging, cutting underbrush into which he was being pushed.

He heard movements ahead. They had Sun! Angrily he stiffened his body against his captor, but the cold metal jammed more piercingly into his spine, and a gun hammer cocked. Wasn't there anything he could do to help his family?

The hand still jammed over his mouth smelled unwashed and slightly oily. Did it belong to a soldier or a thief?

At last brush stopped whipping his face. Where were they? Back on the road?

Aaiee! A light shone directly in his eyes, and he knew he had better not try to shield them. The light dropped and then his father's face was illuminated, then Sun's and Mother's.

"Who are you?" A voice in broken Laotian growled the question.

"We are the Savang family," answered Father.

The light from three flashlights showed a large clearing and six figures in dark jackets and trousers, with hair down to their shoulders. Girls! Most of Tran's fear turned to shock.

"We are sorry," the voice continued. "We thought you were a patrol."

Tran strained to examine their faces. They weren't girls, but boys, about his age. Boys with long hair!

Mother spoke in Hmong. "Your accent ... Are you from the mountains?"

"Yes," one replied in the same language. "We are Hmong."

"Hmong Sky Soldiers," said another, giving what Tran could see was a sweeping bow.

Tran gasped. Sky Soldiers! Everyone knew of the Hmong boys who banded together to escort their people to safety in Thailand, and to fight the Communists with whatever weapons they had. They were heroes to lowlanders like Tran.

It made Tran proud he was part Hmong, and glad his mother had taught him the Hmong language, so he could understand what was being said now.

"We were in the jungle," said a boy who wore the traditional ankle-length skirt of the tribesmen, instead of trousers as did the others. "We followed the direction of the tracers. We discovered that the bullets found their marks. Help us bury the dead." He motioned with his flashlight.

"Mother, you and the girls stay here." Father beckoned to Tran, and they followed two of the Sky Soldiers to the other side of the clearing.

Their light pointed to bodies, crumpled in a bloody heap. It looked like a family. Tran felt sick to his stomach.

"They made a mistake; they built a fire," said the one in the long skirt, who seemed to be the leader. Tran guessed he was around sixteen, because his voice was lower than the others.

"How can they be buried?" Tran's voice was a hoarse whisper.

"Only one way, my brother. With brush."

Tran cringed, but he couldn't let these brave Hmongs know how he felt.

As the mound of banana leaves and branches over the

24

bodies grew larger, so did his nausea. It would rise as a wave on the water, die down, then rise higher. When they finished, he could no longer keep down the waves. He ran into the forest.

Footsteps crackled behind him, and the voice of the oldest Sky Soldier spoke softly.

"It is all right. I did the same, the first time I saw people like this."

Tran's body finished its outcry. He turned, exhausted but grateful for the calmness inside and the compassion of the older boy.

He spoke thickly because his mouth was dry. "I behaved as a baby."

The young soldier offered Tran a canteen and turned off his light. He was quiet for a moment, then said briefly, "You do things that need to be done. Babies do not."

The awful taste in Tran's mouth began to go away. "My name is Tran," he said.

"I am Nao."

Tran handed back the canteen, and Nao grabbed it roughly.

"Do you know, I found my family the way you saw those bodies!" His voice choked. "Father, mother, brothers, sisters. All dead!"

Tran's horror kept him from saying anything. After a moment he ventured a soft question. "Were they also shot?"

Nao gave a forced laugh that ended in a cry. "Not so fast for them. Poison gas. Whole village . . ."

"Everybody?" Tran felt sick again.

"They said they only kill those who resist the Communist take-over." Nao spit out the words. "They are butchers! They *enjoy* killing!" Then Nao's voice seemed to come from a long way away, getting louder and closer until it ended in a muffled roar. "I took a vow over my family's bodies that I will fight Communists. I will drive them from our homeland. I will not cut my hair until we are victorious. If I have to, I will fight alone, while everyone else flees!"

Tran's face was hot with shame. "Do you hate my family for escaping?"

Nao was silent. Then he sighed. "No. The way you speak, I know your family is educated. You would be hunted if you stayed; maybe your fighting will be done someplace else. You must tell people what Communists do when they get in power."

The two boys carefully made their way through the darkness toward the dim glow at the other side of the clearing.

Nao sighed again. "Father wished me to go to school. I only wanted to be a peaceful farmer in the mountains I love. They gave us room for our rice fields, good streams for fish, and big rain forests with game to hunt. Plenty of bamboo. We could move our village and always have enough to build houses."

He stopped walking and reached out to Tran. He clasped his shoulder and said, "Someday, my brother, with help from us both, the peaceful life will return to Laos!"

They were on the other side of the clearing now, where Tran's family and the other Sky Soldiers waited.

"Nao," said one of the boys in a low voice. "They need to get to the river. Could we help them?"

Nao listed to Father's plan to go down the river into the sea.

"There are many daring plans for escape," he said, "but this one is very dangerous. You'll need to get on the other side of the falls, and you will be in Communist territory all the way down river. There will be pirates in the open sea, and then . . . the monsoon."

26

"I know," said Tran's father. "The level of the river will rise so fast when the rain starts that the current will push us right back up river, and maybe into Tonle Sap."

"Yes," agreed Nao. "The Great Lake of Cambodia. I have heard of people being trapped there. If you go, go quickly. We can help you get through the jungle to the river."

"Go," he said to two other boys, "to the ones we left yesterday, who had started for Thailand. See if they would go with the Savangs. If so, tell them to meet us here." Nao squatted on the ground and drew a map in the dust.

The two nodded, then checked their flashlights, canteens and knives, which hung from sashes around their waists. A moment later they were swallowed up by the night and the jungle.

"My men move swiftly," Nao said. "And the other people are closer to our meeting point. We had better leave now. If enough people want a boat, you can leave without delay." He turned to another Sky Soldier. "They need their motor-bicycle. Go back and help them get it."

"We need it too," growled the warrior. "It would buy plenty of ammunition."

A low chorus of voices agreed.

"They won't get out of the country without it," Nao said firmly. "We will give them their possession." He sent another boy, smaller than Tran, back with him for the discarded bicycle.

When they found the motor-bicycle and Tran managed to get it upright again, the boy snarled at him. "You have been to school, and you have money for a motor-bicycle, but you will not stay and fight the Communists. We have to take care of you like babies! Bah!"

Tran watched him spit on the ground, and his face again burned.

As they started back through the maze of vines, Tran asked quietly, "Did you leave your family to fight?"

"I have no family," the boy said defiantly. "My mother and sister were killed by a Communist patrol when we tried to cross the river to Thailand. Now I fight them. I want to *fight*, not take people out of the country. Hmongs don't slither away in the darkness like lizards! We fight, and work like the buffalo. Even if we starve, we will not complain!"

Tran felt a surge of shame. Was he being cowardly to try to escape with his family? Should he stay and fight? But there wasn't time to think about it. They were back in the clearing.

"Nao says we will cut a southwesterly course through the jungle, avoiding all trails," Father said. He took a metal compass from his pocket.

"No," said Nao. "It is shiny. It will reflect in the eyes of a patrol." He reached inside his sash and pulled out a round, dark object. "A compass from an American soldier. He gave it to my uncle," he said proudly. "It does not reflect."

Ahh, thought Tran. Nao's uncle must have been one of the original Sky Soldiers who fought the Communists in the mountains during the Vietnam War. The Americans gave them their name for being so tough and dependable. Tran was impressed.

The line moved out, slowly in order to be quiet. With Nao in front, holding a shaded flashlight and hacking away branches with his large knife, Tran's face didn't take the whipping as before; but the huge blisters formed on both hands from gripping the handlebars were rubbed raw with each lurch and stumble, and brought tears of pain. The rest of his aching body cried out from the vibrations.

After what seemed hours, suddenly the procession halted. The jungle wasn't so thick now, and everything was still, except for the high, chirpy sound of a mongoose. From somewhere in front of them came an answering call.

Within seconds, dry branches crackled and low voices murmured ahead. Tran pushed his way forward. Aided by the glow of a couple of lights, he could see Father, Nao and other men talking softly but excitedly.

Father brought his family together. "We are near the banks of a small port town, nearly on the Cambodian border," he said. "The other group has decided to try our plan. It is almost dawn, so we'll hide and rest here until dusk, then try to get a boat."

Nao joined them. "We must leave. You are close to rice paddies, and the forest isn't thick, so you must either hide in the trees for the day or burrow like this."

He showed them how to scoop away the soft soil with their hands. Then he lay down in the indentation and tried to burrow his body even deeper into the ground. Lastly, he pulled nearby leaves and branches over him like a thick blanket, until only a space remained for breathing.

"The patrols won't search these woods unless they think they have spotted something, so you must stay hidden until darkness comes again."

Then he pulled from his sash a long length of string, which he cut into five pieces.

Mother smiled gently. "My son, we are Christians and don't believe in the spirits."

"But it would make me feel better to give these to you," said Nao as he tied one around Mother's wrist. He tied one around the wrist of each family member, and as he finished Tran's he said, "My brother Tran, the string will keep your protective spirit with you until you arrive safely."

He laid a hand on Tran's shoulder. "Victory! Soon! *Muslawm*, young brother."

"Good-bye," returned Tran, barely able to say it.

The Sky Soldiers disappeared. The string felt tight around Tran's wrist, but he would never take it off. Not because of protective spirits, but because it would remind him of Nao and the Sky Soldiers.

Tran helped dig hiding places for the family, and when he was alone in his burrow to wait out the day he made a promise to himself.

I will never cut my hair until Laos is free. Never. I am a Hmong soldier.

5

The Sky Soldiers' kites whipped through the air. "Come join us," the soldiers called to Tran. "Prove you are a man!"

He heard his kite flutter behind him as it lifted into the sky. But it was night. He couldn't see!

"I can't see the kites!"

"Bah! You are a baby!" Someone spit in his face.

"But I can't see," he sobbed.

"You worry too much." Sy appeared in the blackness, holding the Blue Star. "Your kite has been cut. It must be buried."

Tran sobbed harder. "Please don't bury my Blue Star."

Nao's face emerged. "He has cut his hair. He isn't one of us. Bury them both."

Tran felt brush on top of him. There was no air! He awakened, gasping for breath. Where was he? Leaves fell from his face as he sat up in his shallow gravelike hiding place.

He had been dreaming, or had he? His heart still pounded against his ribs, and he took a few deep breaths trying to slow it, but the air was heavy, and he couldn't get enough into his lungs.

He saw his father and some of the other men climb down from the trees where they had positioned themselves to watch for the enemy. They could hardly stand after being cramped so long. Soon people were milling quietly in the forest.

The nightmare faded and Tran felt calmer, but his

stomach began to hurt and he realized how hungry he was. Mother reached into the food pack and gave him a roll of cold rice. He looked at it in amazement. Was that all? He gulped it down and looked expectantly at her. She silently handed him a *rambuten.*

He held the small red fruit under his nose and pensively moved its hairy surface back and forth across his lips as the sweet aroma filled his head like a pleasant cloud. This was from the tree in the corner of their garden which he would never see again. Maybe there would never be any more juicy *rambutens.* He ate it slowly as he slapped at mosquitoes and watched small clusters of people going past him, out of the forest.

Sun tiptoed over to him and said softly, "Father says people are going into the river village in small groups so they won't attract attention. We . . ." Her sentence ended in spasms of coughing.

Tran reached out his hand to his sister, but saw Father motion that they were leaving. With a backward glance at Sun, who was still coughing, he picked up the motor-bicycle and pack.

"Father," he whispered, "Sun isn't well. Perhaps she should be near you and Mother. Paw can walk with me. It isn't far to the village, is it?"

"Only a few miles," agreed Father. "But I don't want us to be separated." He looked at Sun, who couldn't stop coughing. "However, we can't take her until she is quiet, and with the motor-bicycle you need to go now, so you can see to cross the dikes. Paw also needs to see where she is going." He looked doubtful. "Very well, you and Paw start walking and we will catch up to you. Groups leave every thirty minutes, so we will be that much behind you; but we can travel faster than you."

The forest was growing dim, but they could still see the way. Paw held tightly to the back of the bicycle while Tran guided it carefully through the trees.

When they emerged from the sparse forest, water-covered rice fields glistened in every direction over the flat land. The rim of red sun still left above the horizon cast a glow over the paddies and reminded Tran of the sparkling wares set out by jewelry merchants in the marketplace at home. In the distance a village, perched on stilts, shimmered against a wide band of silver. The Mekong!

He hastened his steps, then remembered Paw. He must go carefully, for her sake. The rice paddies were divided by earthen dikes, solid for walking, but barely wide enough for two to pass. She must not fall in.

Tran walked for some time with his head down to watch her. When he looked up to check their progress, he froze! A few yards ahead was a squad of government soldiers!

Panic-stricken, he looked around. Father and Mother were nowhere in sight. There was no place to turn off, and not enough room to turn the bicycle around. It was too late to escape anyway; the soldiers had already spotted them. A warning shot whistled over their heads as the green uniformed men headed toward them.

Perhaps, thought Tran, they will only think he and Paw were from the village. For the first time, he was thankful he had lost his sandals in the forest. Villagers didn't wear shoes.

He stood still as the five men, carrying rifles with bayonets attached, approached. His heart pounded so loudly, he was sure they could hear it!

"Mama . . ." whimpered Paw as the fierce-looking men came toward them.

"Hush, Paw! Be quiet!" Tran's heart felt as though it would jump out of his body. Where was the courage Father said he would have when he needed it?

33

The leader trained his rifle on them. "What are you doing?" he snarled.

"Sir, we are just going to the village." Tran could hear his shaking voice.

The leader looked them up and down, taking in their dusty, torn clothing, and then the motor-bicycle. His eyes narrowed. "Where did you get that?"

"My sister and I uncovered it in the woods. We are going to sell it."

That was the truth, Tran thought, as he pointed to a section of forest far down from where his parents and the others were.

"We will save you the trouble. Take it!" The second soldier in line started forward at the command.

Tran held tightly to the handlebars. "But . . ."

Before he knew what had happened, the squad leader had stepped around him and roughly picked up Paw by the arms.

A shout of glee went up from the other soldiers. "Bayonet practice," shouted one.

"Let me have her. I can throw higher than you!" yelled another.

The leader laughed cruelly. "I'll throw the brat. You all sharpen your bayonet skills." He laughed again as he looked at the horrified Tran. "This also sharpens cooperation from you villagers."

With that, he hurled the screaming Paw into the air.

"No!" As the outcry tore from his lips, Tran dropped the bicycle and lunged for his little sister.

The soldier whirled his bayonet around toward him, and Tran felt searing pain across his cheek just as Paw's body collided against his chest and upraised arms.

The force of the impact knocked them off the dike into

34

the shallow, muddy water. Paw's head went under, and Tran struggled to keep her upright and to regain his own footing.

From above, he heard a loud oath and a promise to shoot them like ducks.

Then another voice, lower, said something about darkness and more valuables in the forest. "All right!" shouted the first. "They will tell the villagers not to argue!"

Tran was on his knees, his back toward them, hugging Paw tightly to his chest. He held his breath, until he heard them move off across the dikes. Then he cautiously peered around. They were heading for the forest with the motorbicycle, but in the direction he had pointed. Tran was thankful for that.

Holding Paw, he got to his feet. Somehow his pack had stayed strapped to his back, and the weight bore down on him as he battled to climb out of the smelly muck.

Blood streamed from his face onto his mud-caked shirt. His cheek hurt terribly, and he wanted to lie down on the grassy dike, but knew he didn't dare.

Paw hiccuped from the fright and her hard crying. He held her with one hand and pressed the other against his gaping cheek. They must get out of the rice paddies.

By the time they reached the village, Tran staggered from dizziness. The houses closest to the fields seemed to be storage buildings and were deserted. He pulled Paw under one of them and leaned wearily against one of the poles that supported the house.

Paw climbed on his lap, and chickens investigated the reason their feeding ground was disturbed, but Tran didn't know it.

"Son!"

Tran heard the voice from a long way off. He opened

his eyes, and Mother's face came into focus. Her eyes looked strange, all hollow and faraway.

He groaned. "Paw . . ."

"We know, Son. We came from the forest just as Paw was thrown in the air." She closed her eyes. "There was nothing we could do, except hide and wait. We thought we had lost you both." She brushed his forehead with her lips. "You were very brave."

"Yes," agreed Father, who held Paw. "You risked your life for her."

"The motor-bicycle . . ." began Tran.

"We are thankful there was the motor-bicycle for them to take," said Father softly. "Otherwise . . ."

Tran sighed and closed his eyes as Mother gently washed the area around the slash with water from their water bottle. She placed a clean compress over it and then wound a long strip of cloth around and around his head, to hold the compress in place.

"The bleeding will stop soon," she said.

Tran winced. It hurt!

"Come!" said Father urgently. "Everyone will be at the river by now."

Tran's knees shook as he pulled himself to his feet. What good would it do to go to the river? They wouldn't have enough money to persuade an official to take the risk of helping them escape. They were trapped!

He looked at Sun to see if her face betrayed the same feeling, but she seemed tired and withdrawn. Her coughing! Was she really ill?

The village's dim street was filled with people shopping in open marketplaces. It surprised Tran, because at home markets were open only during the day. They passed vendors selling chunks of barbecued pork and eggplant, skewered on bamboo sticks. Tran's mouth watered. Another vendor called to the family, "Come try my tasty *orlam*."

That was Tran's favorite stew. The spicy smell of the grouse meat and buffalo skin, flavored with sandalwood, drifted enticingly from the seller's cart. It made him feel light-headed from hunger.

Oh, if they could only stop for something to eat! But he knew they didn't dare take the time, nor spend the money.

The wharf also teemed with people. Fishermen prepared nets or tried selling fish caught that morning. The stench from rotten fish, left too long in the heat, made Sun cover her nose and mouth.

A man in a blue government uniform stood with his back to them, as he watched the busy docks. Father stood behind him and said softly, "We have need of boat passage."

The man didn't turn around. "To what destination?"

"Down the Mekong."

Tran gasped. Would the official immediately call for soldiers?

But the man didn't move. "To send a ship that far is a great risk for me to take."

Father placed the money pouch in his hands and whispered something.

The man shook his head. "Too great a risk."

Tran's heart sank. There wasn't enough money! They needed the motor-bicycle and he had lost it! Now they could never escape, and it was all his fault. Scalding tears stung his eyes. Then a resolve settled over him. He would sacrifice himself!

"Sir," he said quietly, "if my family may have passage, I will stay and . . . and be your servant the rest of my life."

"No!" gasped Mother.

"Father, Mother . . ." Tran scarcely recognized the steeliness in his own voice. "You have taught that I must someday give an account of myself. When I do, I wish to stand with Pastor Oh."

"No . . ." began Father.

But the official, without moving, interrupted. "This Pastor Oh. He is Chinese?"

"Ye—es," said Father.

"Ahh." The government man turned to look at the family. He was Chinese! "I met Pastor Oh during the Vietnamese purge of the Chinese. I am Buddhist, but he risked his life to keep my wife and me alive." He put the pouch of money in his coat and pulled out a paper which he handed to Father. "Go. Your boat is there." He indicated his head toward a small freighter a few yards away. "Hurry." He turned his back again.

"Walk fast." Father wasted no more time in covering the distance to the ship. He showed the paper to a guard, and the family hurried up the gangplank, just as the captain directed it to be pulled up.

People sat everywhere on the dirty deck, invisible to anyone on the dock. Father found space next to some heavy ropes and motioned his family to sit down. They collapsed, too weary to move any farther.

Tran gazed through burning eyes at the unfamiliar surroundings. Would he have been brave enough to stay while his family left? And Pastor Oh. What a privilege that they had been allowed to know him. That was something even a whole troop of soldiers couldn't take away!

He looked into the dark sky as a single star flashed out. *Good-bye, my country. Good-bye, star. If I live, I will return. I will, I . . .*

Tran fell asleep.

6

A change in the steady vibration of the ship's engines awakened Tran. The instant he opened his eyes, he knew two things: they had made it onto the ship, and his cheek throbbed.

He wanted to stand up. Was that permissible? He eased to his feet, feeling a rush of warmth in his legs as the blood circulated more freely.

The night's blackness hid the deck and most of its inhabitants, but here and there unseen sprawled figures gave off snores.

A moving form, low to the deck, caught his attention. It came closer, then stood up as it reached him.

"It's good you are awake, Son." Father kept his voice low enough so only Tran could hear it. "I have talked to the captain. He feels it's best to let everyone sleep, but has need of extra ears for the next hour or two."

"Why? Where are we?" whispered Tran.

"We have gone about 150 kilometers, and are deep into Cambodia."

Tran's throat tightened.

"The night has so far been uneventful, but we will soon reach a spot where the Mekong joins another river. There is a town nearby. The captain cut the engines so we will not be heard." Father tapped Tran's arm. "Come. The captain wishes two men to stand on the bridge to listen and watch. Don't try to walk. You will trip over someone."

Tran crawled behind Father, one hand outstretched for obstacles. Once he crawled over what he thought was the top part of an anchor, only to discover it was someone's leg! "I'm sorry," he mumbled as he hastily went around it.

A moment later he batted away what he thought was the fringe of a dangling rope.

"Uumph!" said an old man's sleepy voice. "What is going on with my beard?"

Tran was glad to hear Father whisper, "Here are the steps to the bridge. Hold on."

It was quiet on top of the ship. Tran couldn't hear the rumble of the engines as he had on the deck. To the left of where he and his father stood was a large room lighted only by the soft glow from instrument panels. Three men hunched over them intently.

"There are rapids and shallow places through here." Father spoke quietly in Tran's ear. "The crew must pay attention to the depth-finder and other controls. Our task is to be alert for anyone who has spotted us."

Tran gripped the railing in front of him and tried to see through the darkness. He listened, but the only sound was a low roar he hadn't noticed before.

"What is that?" he whispered.

"The exhaust. They can't lower its noise."

"Oh." A lump rose in Tran's throat. The exhaust might be heard by Communists on shore.

Hours passed, and in the east a faint streak of pink replaced the stars. Tran bent first one knee and then the other, trying to rest his legs.

In the silence and darkness of night, he knew a kerosene lamp a mere half-mile away would have looked bright. But he hadn't even seen that, much less lights indicating a town.

Of course Cambodia didn't have real towns any more. "Our neighbor, Cambodia, has just been conquered by their Communists, the Khmer Rouge," his teacher had announced in hushed tones last year. That wasn't of importance in the minds and lives of Tran and his friends—until now. Now he understood.

The captain emerged from the wheelhouse. "So far, all right. Now everyone must go into the holds for the daylight hours."

"The holds!" exclaimed Father. "But isn't there cargo down there?"

The captain snorted. "Cargo and all of you? We ride low in this fresh warm water anyway. Any more weight and she would draw so much water we would touch the bottom of the Mekong!"

Father nodded. "Then for our safety, it's wise we stay in the holds."

"Your safety," barked the captain, "is not important to me. But I don't want the Communists to think I'm carrying anything but cargo. Get everyone below!"

A crewman went with Tran and his father to help round up the refugees. Soon a jumble of sleepy, crying children, bewildered grandparents, packs and mats were crowded down the hatches into the holds.

"It's so dark!" wailed Sun. "Why can't we be in sunshine?" She began to cough.

"Shh, child." Mother put both arms around her. "We can stand darkness for awhile longer." A dim light went on overhead, and Mother looked up at it as though it were a thing of beauty. "Now we'll be able to see each other and talk to each other for the first time in many days."

She sat down on the cold metal floor and yanked the edge of her skirt from under someone who was going to sit on it. Seeming not to notice the hubbub of the people jammed around them, she arranged herself as best she could and said, "Tran, let me look at your wound. Then everyone will tell a story."

The day dragged on, and the heat was now stifling. The small amount of air from the opening to the deck didn't help. Tran's clothes were soaked with perspiration, he was thirsty, and his head felt as though it floated on someone else's body. The rice roll and *rambuten* that Mother passed around didn't help the gnawing pain in his stomach.

The family sitting next to them had finished their meager meal when the man pulled from his pack something that looked like a spiny hand grenade.

"Oh, no!" exclaimed Sun, who had seen it too. "A *durian*!"

Several people around tried to move away, but couldn't. Tran smiled. Sy enjoyed eating strong-smelling *durians*, but when he brought one to school several boys demanded he sit apart from them.

"My friend," said Father, "I like the *durian*, but for the sake of those who don't, perhaps you could wait until we are again on deck to open it."

"What do you mean?" retorted the man indignantly. "The *durian* is the sweetest gift on earth to the taste buds. And I may eat what I like!" With a flourish, he whacked the fruit open.

In no time at all, cries from the shadows—"Oh, no! Who has a *durian*?"—mixed with gagging sounds. Sun put both hands over her face and turned to the wall.

Just then, the captain came down the ladder. "What in the name of river-boats is that terrible smell? A *durian*? Who would be stupid enough to open one of those in a crowded place!" He climbed back up a few steps, then shouted, "It's growing dark. You may come on deck."

Tran didn't know when he had seen people move so fast, and when the man who had eaten the *durian* joined them on top, no one wanted to sit beside him.

Father went up to the bridge to talk to the captain. When he returned, he said, "We have been fortunate. Military installations haven't yet been set up on the flat land along the river, but the captain is concerned because soon we'll be in the south, near the city of Phnom Penh. There will be military units in that area. He wishes several men to be on guard tonight. Enjoy a little sleep now, Son, and then stand watch with me."

Tran spread his mat on the hard deck, lay down, and looked at the sky. A brisker wind than usual was blowing; it ruffled his hair and brushed his face. Just before he fell asleep he whispered, "Twice today Father called you a man."

7

"Owww!"

Something pelted Tran's face, penetrating through the bandage to his wound.

"Owww!" He leaped to his feet and grabbed at the base of a mast. It took an instant to decide what was happening. By that time, muffled exclamations rose in chorus around the deck.

"Rain!"

"The rains are here!"

"The monsoon season has begun!"

"Rain!"

Others scrambled to their feet around him, and although he couldn't see them clearly, he could tell they lifted thirsty faces to the dark sky. His cheek throbbed from the sting of the hard rain, but he let the swollen drops burst on his forehead and welcomed the soothing wetness that cascaded down his parched face and body. He opened his mouth and tasted the sweet, sweet water.

After a few minutes, he again became aware of his surroundings. Sun was coughing, making deep, hoarse sounds that seemed to come from her toes.

"Mother, I'll help you get Sun and Paw below."

Mother held on to Tran's arm to keep from falling on the slippery deck as they made their way past invisible wire ropes and winches.

He left his pack with them and went up to find Father. The excitement over the rain hadn't decreased.

"First bath in many weeks." A man who was scrubbing himself with his hands laughed when Tran bumped into him.

Tran clung to the rail as he climbed the metal bridge steps. A crew member blocked his way, but stepped aside when he recognized Tran.

"Everyone is happy about the rain, Father," Tran said to the soaked figure illuminated by the wheelhouse's glow. "It feels good to have the dust and mud washed away."

Father wiped the water from his face. "It's refreshing. However, I wish it had waited one day longer until we were out of the river."

Tran started to ask why. Then he remembered. The current would change with the river's rise! "But, Father, this is a fast ship. Can't we get to the sea in time?" Tran had to talk loudly over the noise of the rain.

"To get this far without detection, the captain cut back the engines. We are only going about eight knots an hour, which isn't . . ."

A crackling sound from the wheelhouse interrupted Father, followed by excited voices. Tran strained to hear, but couldn't tell what they said.

A sailor hurried out. "What is the excitement?" Father asked. "May we be of assistance?"

"We are close to the city of Phnom Penh. They have radioed us to identify ourselves and come into port!" The sailor's voice grew shriller with each word.

The familiar lump of fear settled in Tran's stomach, while the rain beat on the metal bridge like millions of tiny footsteps.

Father spoke. "Tell the captain we will get the people down into the holds. I'll return to help in any other way."

Happy voices rose from the bow to the stern of the boat, as Tran and Father reached the deck. Then one after another lapsed into silence as the news Father spoke to a few spread. The passengers made their way to the hatches and down into the dark, stuffy holds.

"You, too, Son."

"But, Father—"

"I wish you to be down here to take care of your mother and sisters, in case something happens to me." Father's voice was very quiet.

"But isn't there something I can do now?" Tran felt tears sting the back of his eyes. "I wish to help fight."

Father was abrupt. "You may do your fighting as a warrior of prayer. That is our need now."

The small overhead light in the hold showed sixty or seventy dripping people. Soaked clothes were plastered against bodies. There was no place to spread out to dry, so they squatted on the floor. Tran thought each one looked like an island in the midst of a huge water puddle.

But most didn't seem to mind being uncomfortable, he thought. What he saw on faces was fear. After all they had been through, was this the way their journey was to end, taken prisoners by the Cambodians?

The hatch cover banged shut, and a few minutes later the overhead light went out. The instant blackness was thick and smothery. A stifled gasp arose from the dark. Children began to cry and were hushed by parents.

"Now we can't even see what our fate is to be," mumbled Tran. "Not until the soldiers take us out one by one. Or maybe they'll throw a bomb down here to save themselves further bother."

He buried his head between his knees. He wasn't sure he was a very good prayer warrior, but he would try.

Time stretched on. Tran thought it was like sending the Blue Star into the night sky. It went on and on, but he couldn't tell how far or where it was. Had hours gone by, or only minutes?

The perspiring bodies and wet clothes of so many people jammed together blended into a choking smell. Sun coughed again. Oh, would this never end?

Just when Tran thought he couldn't stand it any longer, the small light went on, the hatch opened, and Father stood on the steps.

"Friends," he said in a tired voice, "we have passed Phnom Penh safely."

Excited cries greeted this statement.

Father held up his hand. "The captain radioed the Cambodians that we weren't receiving their message well, and that we are heading to a Vietnam port for repairs. They apparently thought we were a Vietnamese ship, for they said no more about identifying ourselves. They are contacting the next Vietnamese port to tell them we are coming."

A groan went up.

"We shall face that problem when it arises," Father went on. "Meanwhile, since it will be about six hours before we reach there, the captain says we may go on deck in shifts. The rain has stopped."

People talked among themselves as to who should go in the first shift, but the man who had eaten the *durian* elbowed his way to Father.

"We pass the Cambodians, only now to let the Vietnamese take us prisoner?" he bellowed. "The Vietnamese Communists started all our troubles. I demand a boat be put over the side so my family can go ashore here!"

Tran saw Father lay a hand on the man's shoulder. "Friend, come up here, so we can talk."

The two disappeared up on deck. Tran couldn't even guess what Father said, but when the man returned he seemed calm and deep in thought.

Tran's shift was last, but he didn't mind. Now there was room to move around, and with the hatch cover open, good air to breathe.

"Is there anything to eat?" he asked Mother.

"The rice is all gone," she said dismally. "There is only a little fruit left." She handed him a green orange. They were usually sweeter than the orange-colored ones that came into season during the monsoons. This one, though, was rotting.

Tran ate all of the good part. The skin was tangy and stung his mouth, which had been parched by dust. He looked at the squishy brown section, sighed, and put that in his mouth too. It wouldn't kill him, and it was one more bite to put in his hollow stomach.

He stretched out full length, with his head pillowed on his pack. A thought occurred to him. He opened the pack, rummaged until he found the object in the center, and without unwrapping it probed the surface until he was satisfied. A smile played on his lips. Mother's plate had come this far unbroken. That was a good sign.

His smile faded. Or would it end up in Vietnamese hands?

He looked out of the corner of his eye at Mother. Had she been eating anything? Her round face had hollows, and her smooth forehead was now wrinkled as she tried to get Sun to eat part of an orange. He remembered how her eyes had looked as he came back to consciousness under that house. He searched for something to say. "We'll be out of the river soon, Mother," he said. "Then we'll get a physician for Sun. It will be all right."

Mother reached out and stroked his damp hair. She nodded, then said, "We must check your wound after awhile."

When it was time for his shift, Tran rushed to find Father. The same hard-driving rain was coming down again.

He jumped as the engines below set up a clamor. "What's happening?" he shouted.

Father shouted back, "The river is already rising. The captain has to put the engines at full throttle if we are to make it in time."

"But the Vietnamese!" Father couldn't hear him, so Tran pointed down river. Father shook his head and turned back to his watch.

The rain stopped after awhile. A faint pink appeared in the east, and the clouds scudded away to regroup for another attack. At least it seemed that way to Tran.

He watched a sailor hoist a flag. It had a big yellow star in the center. Tran guessed it was Vietnamese.

He stood shivering beside Father as the sun rose and touched the green shores lightly settled with houses on stilts. He wondered about the people living there, but his eyes burned and his cheek throbbed, making it hard to think very long. A smell of charcoal drifted from the bank, and here and there war-defoliated trees shamefully bared themselves.

"Do you wish to go below?" Father asked softly.

Tran was surprised to be given the choice. He blinked his eyes hard. "Not just yet."

The Mekong was already heavy with brown silt, and Tran gazed sadly at the sight of palm and mango trees struggling against the rising river. Leafy branches, bent by the coffee-colored current, strained to right themselves.

It is of no use, he said silently to them. *You will all be eventually drowned. But maybe some of you will be strong enough to stand again after being beaten down.* He wished he could come back when the water receded, to see.

The early morning sun was hot. Tran sat cross-legged on the bridge, allowing the rays to warm him and dry his clothes. He was comfortable and drowsy, but he wished the sun's reflection on the glistening water wasn't so bright. The glare bounced into his tired eyes in a staccato fashion. He started to shield them, but Father pulled him to his feet and pointed.

"Look, Morse code."

The captain emerged from the wheelhouse with a large round light. He blinked it on and off a few times, then waited. "The sons of dogs at the signal station tell us to identify ourselves or they'll send out a patrol boat," he sputtered.

"What did you tell them?" Father asked.

The captain snorted. "I told them to repeat the message! It's a delaying tactic." He kept his eyes on the signals flashing from shore. "Perhaps if we time it right, we can be past their reaches before they get a boat readied." He sighed. "Perhaps."

The bright flashes stopped, and as the captain responded with his blinker light he muttered, "We fly your flag, you crawlers of earth. That's all you'll get from us!"

As he finished his signal, he spat into the river. "With luck, those sheep won't realize until too late that the next port can't handle the repairs I told them we needed. Full speed ahead," he shouted to the man at the wheel.

"But, sir," the helmsman protested, "we are at full speed. The current is strong."

"Then it will take luck," said the captain as he looked back at more flashes from shore.

Tran and Father exchanged glances. Tran knew his father was thinking that it would take something more.

They waited. Ominous black clouds began to creep into the blue sky. Tran shivered.

"There they are," the captain said suddenly.

Tran squinted. A flash of light moved out from the shore and headed down river toward the ship.

"No need to hide the people in the holds." The captain shook his head. "We'll be searched. Just make them sit down on deck so they won't be seen from the patrol boat. Cursed dogs!" he shouted, shaking his fist at the oncoming speedboat.

Tran started down the steps to pass the word. For some reason, the knot of fear wasn't there. He was thinking about someplace he could hide his mother and sisters.

All at once a blanket of rain came down. It hit the water so hard the drops bounced back up, white, like pearls strewn over a cinnamon sea. It sent those on deck scurrying for cover—in the hold, under dirty tarps, wherever they could find it.

I didn't have to say anything, Tran said to himself. *Everyone is already hidden from view*!

The captain looked through his binoculars at the patrol boat and chortled. "Those lily-livered curs are turning around!" He shook his fist toward them again. "Next time, put a roof on your boat and you'll be worth something to your demented government! Hah, hah!"

Father reached out his arms and hugged Tran. "The hardest rain I have ever seen came just in time."

"But," worried Tran, "won't there be more patrol boats down river?"

"It's possible," answered the captain, "but that will be the Mekong Delta. There is a maze of over 4,000 kilometers of connecting waterways. The major ones to the capital city of Saigon are usually the only ones patrolled."

He went into the wheelhouse, slapped the crewmen on the back, then stuck his head back out in the rain. His smile had disappeared. "Then we'll have other things to worry about."

Tran and Father went into the dry hold to tell Mother the news. She smiled faintly, then handed them each a half rotten orange.

"This is all the food there is. I have saved a bit for Sun when she wakes up." She passed her hand over the flushed face of the sleeping girl. Every few minutes Sun's whole body would shake with her coughing, but she didn't awaken.

This time Tran didn't stop to even look at the spoiled part of the fruit. It was all food, something to quiet his stomachache.

He went up on deck. The rain had stopped, and the sky was clearing. For a long time he listlessly watched the surging water as it pushed its way over nearly drowned islands and rocked the boats of the few fishermen he saw silhouetted in the afternoon sun.

The land was flat and the shores thickly fringed with palm trees, of a different kind than grew inland. *They must be coconut palms*, he thought. The vision of coconut meat and the thick sweet water inside was almost more than he could stand. They couldn't even slow their frantic journey long enough to net fish swimming under them.

It seemed they were constantly exchanging one problem for two larger ones. The captain said there would be other things to worry about. What were they?

Without warning, the land on either side ended. The ship sailed smoothly over a long roll of white surf and entered a golden world. Tran gasped. There was no turning back now. They were in the South China Sea!

8

Tran spent that night on deck, curled on a rusty piece of canvas. His family was in the hold, caring for Sun, but he wanted to look up at the dark sky awhile.

"Come down when it rains," Mother had cautioned anxiously. "It isn't good to get wet in the night air."

She treats me like a child! That was Tran's first thought, but as he looked at her drawn face he only said, "Yes, Mother, don't worry."

When he went up on deck, the sun's glow was gone and night had already flung a dark banner in the east. As he watched, a jeweled band of stars fitted itself against the blackness. The sight was so beautiful, he almost forgot why they were on this fugitive boat, or that Sun was sick, or that his face hurt. The stars and the huge yellow-orange moon were his friends, and under their watchful eyes he slept.

Toward dawn, conversation between crew members awakened Tran.

"Barometer's falling," said one.

"Storm in a few hours," agreed the other.

Tran got up and went to the hold, where he stumbled over sleeping people. He felt awful. The entire side of his face around the wound stung and throbbed.

He squeezed in beside his family. Mother was trying to give Sun a bit of orange.

"But I'm not hungry," said Sun in a weak voice.

Mother sighed and turned a tired face to Tran.

"May I have ointment for my face?" he asked. "It hurts."

"Aaah," she murmured after unwrapping the bandage. "It's red and swollen with infection. We haven't been as careful as we should."

She looked doubtful. "I don't think our ointment will help. We need something strong."

"I'll see what the captain has," said Father.

When he returned, he carried a bottle half-filled with a liquid Tran didn't recognize.

Father held it up and squinted at it. "This is the alcohol the captain drinks," he said. "But it was the only thing he had to kill the infection in your cheek."

He squatted down to look at Tran. "This will hurt, Son, but it's important to kill the infection. Do you understand?"

Tran silently nodded.

A man sitting next to them joined the conversation. "I'll hold your son down for you," he offered.

Father bowed toward the man. "Thank you, but Tran is a man. He won't need to be held."

Tran swallowed hard and kept his eyes on the floor. He wouldn't disgrace Father. He would not!

As gently as he could, Father spread open the crusted-over wound, then poured the alcohol on Tran's cheek.

Tran yelled, then clenched his fists as the full force of the stinging pain set in. Tears came to his eyes, and he lowered his head and sobbed.

Paw laid her small hand on his arm. "Twan not cwy," she quivered.

After awhile the agony lessened, and he raised his head. Father patted his shoulder, then took a small piece of rotten orange and disappeared on deck.

"You have a strong spirit," said the man who had offered to hold him. "I had that done to me once, and I fought and screamed like a tiger!"

Tran bowed and went up on deck. His head ached from the pain, and he needed air. He found Father unraveling strands from an old piece of rope.

"It's to catch food," he said in answer to Tran's puzzled look.

That's strange, thought Tran. *I've been with Father much in the last two days and nights, but I haven't noticed that his eyes look sunken or that his face has hollows.*

Aloud, he asked, "Do you mean fish?"

Father pulled a strand free. "Some of the men will try to fish, but that may not work well from our height and speed." He looked up at the seabirds circling the ship. "We need food, so we go after something we know we can catch."

Eat a scavenger bird? Tran made a face, then thought better of it. The ache in his stomach had numbed, but he knew that if they didn't eat, they would die. Suddenly the gulls flying overhead looked like a delicious banquet.

Father bent one end of a short length of wire into an open hook. He made the other end into a closed circle, threaded the rope strand through it, and tied a knot. He attached a bit of the rotten orange to the hook, and, swinging his fishing line like a lasso, sent it sailing over the stern of the ship.

A sharp-eyed bird swooped down on the bait and was hooked. Tran pulled it in. Within a short period of time, he and Father snared several of the greedy scavengers.

Cleaning them took longer. Tran had never plucked a bird before, and when he finally finished one he was dismayed to find that most of the bird disappeared with the feathers!

The captain had warned everyone not to ask the crew for food, but they could use the small galley stove to cook what they had. As a result, there were always at least five people waiting to use it. Tran and Father waited patiently for the line to move. When they got to the stove, they discovered the large galley pot hadn't been washed for a long time. It was scummy and smelly.

"Your mother wouldn't like us to cook in such a thing," grimaced Father.

He went to the end of the line, to wait another turn, while Tran took the pot on deck and tried to clean it with a little seawater that stood in a barrel. He wished Mother were here to help him. He wasn't good at cleaning dishes. At home, either she or Sun did that, and when he married, his wife would; so he had never seen any need to learn the art.

When he returned to the galley, Father (who had again progressed to the head of the line) examined the pot and shook his head. "It will have to do." He filled it with rainwater that had been caught in another barrel, plopped in the birds, and waited for them to boil.

Tran supposed the birds would be like the fat, flavorful grouse Mother put in the *orlam*, but these had little meat and tasted fishy. However, it was food, and as the family sucked the bones clean, he wished they had more. Only two birds were left.

The *durian* man walked over and squatted down beside them. "Many pardons for the intrusion," he bowed, "but I wonder if you would be so kind as to give one of those birds to my family? Our food ran out, and I was unable to catch any fish. My children are very hungry."

Father glanced at Mother, then stood, and with a bow to the man proffered a bird. "Please be so kind to take our humble offering."

After many thanks, the man left. Tran couldn't contain himself. "Father, that man has been so disagreeable!"

Father moved the sea-gull bones into a pile. "Son, we nourish our bodies with food, but we nourish our souls with kindness."

Tran said no more, but he still wasn't certain he would have given that man the food for which they had worked so hard.

When he went over to watch some men throwing dice, he learned more about one of the problems the captain had mentioned.

"Have you seen signs yet of pirates?" one asked another.

"No, but I hear the captain is worried."

"And well he ought to be," another said. "They have caught many boats, stripped them of valuables, abused the women and children, and then set fire to the boats. Why, I heard . . ."

Tran walked away. Were they telling the truth? He rested his arms on the rusty rail and stared absently at the water. The waves had caught sunbeams and seemed to be playing with them, tossing them back and forth from one to another. It reminded Tran of a game he used to play in the schoolyard with Sy and the other boys.

If he thought hard, perhaps the past week would disappear and he would be back at school with Blue Star and his friends.

He didn't know how long he had stared at the water when he noticed it no longer sparkled. It was darkening. The air suddenly felt heavy and hot. He looked up. The birds had disappeared. Black clouds stood poised on the edge of the horizon and, as he watched, moved purposefully toward the ship.

The captain hurried by and pointed to them. "We're in for it now!"

9

A light breeze rippled the water and soon stroked Tran's face. After a few minutes, the breeze turned into a steady wind, and drops of rain spattered down.

Everyone scurried to the hold, but Tran continued to watch. A storm would at least break the monotony.

He jumped as a blue flash arced overhead. Then the heavens seemed to explode with a sound like ripping cloth, amplified thousands of times.

A crewman rushed by and glared at Tran. "The captain says everyone must go below!" he shouted.

Tran clamped his hands over his ears as another thunderclap bounced from the sky. He lurched his way across the rolling deck and half slid into the hold.

The light bulb's glow faded in and out as it swung from its dangling cord and illuminated the people on the floor, trying in vain to keep from sliding into each other as the ship slanted up, then down, then rolled to one side, then the other.

As the wallowing, plunging ship groaned and creaked, Tran pictured it breaking up, throwing everyone into the sea, into the mouths of hundreds of hungry sharks.

The man next to him got seasick, and Tran tried to squeeze away from him. He felt sick himself in the stifling air and motioned to his father that he wished to go on deck. Father, who looked pale, got unsteadily to his feet. He was going too.

Wind and water hit them after they succeeded in pushing open the hatch.

"I know nothing about storms at sea. I think we shouldn't have come up here." Father's voice was barely audible.

Braced against the wind, a sudden violent pitch caught Tran unprepared, and he was thrown halfway down the tilted deck.

"Grab hold of something!" Father shouted as he held on to the base of a boom.

Tran's arms flailed around, finally closing over a heavy iron frame. He linked his arms tight, just before a wall of angry green foam smashed over him. He sputtered and gasped.

"Father!" he yelled.

Father made his way to him. "I didn't know it would be this bad!" he shouted in Tran's ear. "We're closer to the wheelhouse than the hold opening. We must try to get up there!"

Hand over hand, clutching wires and ropes, they inched their way toward the bridge steps. Tran stared in horror at each mountain of water that towered, broke and washed over the deck. They could be swept into the sea like insects!

In the driving rain, he couldn't tell who came from the wheelhouse to help them up, and the captain's voice seemed a long way off when he told them to go down the ladder to the engine room.

At least it was dry down there. Tran's teeth chattered as icy water streamed down his body onto the floor.

A crewman, busy checking gauges on the noisy engines, tossed over two oily rags. After Father dried himself and bowed his thanks, he shouted to the man, "I suppose the ship runs at high speed through the big waves."

The crewman's eyes didn't leave the gauges as he shook his head. "The engines turn slowly," he shouted back.

"Why?" yelled Tran, wiping the smelly rag over his hair. "Is something wrong?"

"The lower the speed, the easier she rides with the waves," explained the captain, who had come up behind him. "So we cut back the engines." He squeezed by them to talk to the machinist. "The wind has died down, and so will the waves. It won't be necessary to pour oil on the water."

"Oil?" whispered Tran.

"Have I not told you," whispered back Father, "that kind words calm anger? Oil calms angry water."

"Oh," Tran said. He was disappointed that they wouldn't pour oil on the sea. He would have liked to watch that.

Almost as fast as the old ship had begun its violent ride, the floor under Tran's feet stopped rolling. Father loosened his hold on the water pipe he had been gripping. "The sea must be quiet now," he said.

Suddenly the captain's voice roared into the speaking tube that connected with the pilot house. "I said to increase speed!"

"They can't," objected the machinist. "The cooling intake seems to be clogged, probably with seaweed from the gale. If we increase speed, the engines will heat up!"

"I can't risk lowering any of the crew under the water to see what is clogging it," stormed the captain. "So until we dock, we must travel as the sea cucumber."

He turned to Tran and his father with an angry look. "You were stupid to come up on deck! Get back where you belong!" He stalked ahead of them up to the wheelhouse.

Tran spread out the wet cloth to dry and followed behind. "I think the captain needs oil poured on him," he muttered.

The next morning, Tran half-heard the sounds of waking around him. He turned over on his stomach and threw his arms over his ears to keep out the noise. But people, rolling up mats, kept jostling him, and soon he gave up.

There hadn't been much sleep in their corner of the hold. Sun coughed all night, and Mother made many trips to the communal water barrel to wet cooling cloths for the youngster's hot face.

Tran yawned. "May I go on deck?"

"Yes," answered Father. "I'll go up later, and we'll try catching more birds."

Tran shrugged. His stomach had long ago stopped hurting, and he didn't care if he ate or not. He went up into the pale, gray morning and rubbed the sleep from his eyes.

The ship seemed almost to be stopped, it went so slowly. The steady drone of the engines sounded strange, as though the engines breathed heavily. At this pace, would they ever reach land?

He leaned on the railing and watched a flying fish leap from the water. Its dark form was silhouetted for a split second against the brightening sky, before it dove cleanly back into the depths.

It would be fun to know how to swim, thought Tran. Or to leap into the air. He didn't think the captain would like his jumping on the ship. Had it been just a week since he last ran and laughed with his friends? It seemed like years.

He sighed. There was no one on board his age to talk to. It had been nice talking to Nao. Tran fingered the dirty string bracelet. He knew his parents didn't like him to keep it on his wrist, but it was important to him. Maybe sometime he would remove it, but he would always keep it.

He gazed in the direction they had come from. The Sky Soldiers were back there. What were they doing right now? Suddenly the captain's voice boomed into his thoughts.

"Curse the luck! It's those sons of Thai dogs!"

Tran looked in the direction of the voice. What was the captain talking about?

Then a woman standing nearby cried out, "There are the pirates!" She began to wail. "We'll all be killed!"

10

Tran shielded his eyes from the sun and searched the line between water and sky. All he could see were swells and sun crystals bouncing off the blue water. Wait! A black dot crested on one of the swells. That must be it! He dashed to the hold.

"A pirate ship? Is the captain certain?"

"He said so!" Tran said breathlessly.

Father lost no time in joining the captain, while Tran kept his eyes on the black speck.

When Father returned, he said to Tran and the cluster of men who gathered around, "There are about eight people on a small ship. I suggested they may be friendly Malays, but the captain is sure they are pirates."

The group murmured nervously.

Tran's heart beat faster. He remembered the conversation he had heard about pirates.

One of the men spoke up. "We travel so slowly, they are certain to catch us!"

"They will at this speed," replied Father. "That is why I volunteered to go down and see what is the matter with the engine cooling intake."

The old lump of fear grew in Tran's throat. Under the water? "Let one of the crew go down, Father."

"No, Son. Each of the crew is needed to get this boat to Malaysia. We can't afford an accident to them. I will only be about one and a half meters under the water."

"B. . .but. . ." Tran looked around frantically at the group of men. Each looked away.

"There is no time to stand here." Father's voice rose. "Tran, run tell your mother what I must do, then make haste back here. I wish my son to hold the rope that supports me."

When Tran returned, his father was already climbing over the side of the ship, down an old rope ladder, with another rope tied around his chest.

"He will pull once on the rope when he needs to come up for air, and twice when he wants to be pulled aboard," a crew member said as he anchored the rope around one of the iron castings that lined the side of the hull. "The captain stopped the engines for five minutes while your father works down there. But then we start up again, and he may not get back on board in time."

His heart pounding, Tran leaned over the side and caught the rope that suspended his father between life and death. He held it tighter, while Father's head disappeared beneath the murky water.

One tug for air, two to come up, he repeated to himself.

There was frenzied activity around him. "Women and children, get below. Men, round up every weapon you can lay your hands on," shouted one of the men who had earlier talked of pirates.

Some men pulled knives from packs, while others searched the deck for sharp or heavy things they could use.

Tran felt a sharp tug on the rope. He pulled hard and wound the rope around the casting. Father broke the surface of the water, took a deep breath, and signaled to be lowered again.

"Hurry! They are gaining on us!" shouted someone.

Tran glanced up at a touch on his shoulder. Mother stood beside him, holding her long pair of scissors.

"Mother! This isn't the place for you!"

"Son, this *is* the place for me." She stood very straight,

her face expressionless. "The pirates must get past me to get to your sisters."

Tran stared at her. This wasn't the way she was at home! He turned back to the rope as he felt a tug. Father gulped for air, then disappeared again beneath the water.

Tran looked back. The pirate boat was gaining. He could see dark figures moving about. His throat tightened and he grasped the rope so tightly his scraggly fingernails cut into the flesh of his palms.

Father, please come up. Please hurry, he begged silently. As in response, there came the awaited double tug on the rope. "Help me!" he shouted, and one of the ship's crew ran to help pull Father over the side, but not before Mother grabbed the rope and pulled with all her might.

"It's all right," Father gasped. "Opening . . . clogged . . . seaweed. All right." And he fell to the deck in a spasm of coughing.

"Full speed!" the captain called, and Tran nearly shouted as he heard the engines respond with their full roar. That was the loveliest sound in the world.

Father shook from the water's chill, and someone brought a blanket to wrap around him. As Tran helped him stand, he worried at Father's pale, exhausted face. Just then a yell went up from the men standing silently at the rail, their knuckles showing white from the fierce grip on their weapons.

"We're pulling ahead!"

Tran's heart leaped. Could they outrun the pirates?

Then another cry came. "It's dropping back!"

Tran rushed to look. Sure enough, the pirate ship already was barely visible against the rim of the sea.

"She's wheeled around!" called the captain, lowering his spy glass. "We made it!"

"Yow!" Tran cried, raising both hands in the air.

"That was close," said one of the men. "A few minutes more, and we would have been in their hands. We are grateful." And he bowed toward Tran's father.

Father, still trembling with cold, nodded wearily, and as the rest of the men went to the hold to tell their families the story, he leaned against Mother, and they also walked slowly to the hatchway.

That afternoon there were only two seabirds in the kettle Tran put on to boil. Father was still exhausted, and Tran had been confident he could catch their food. But somehow, today he didn't have the quick reflexes he had before. One bird grabbed the precious bait and flew away.

"It's all right," Father said. "I am too tired to eat."

So Tran and Paw divided the birds, because Mother said she also was too tired, and Sun ate hardly anything anymore.

As Paw put the bones in a small pile to save for soup, everyone in the hold was startled to hear an excited voice call from the deck, "Land! Land ahead!"

The news started a stampede to the hatchway, as everyone tried to squeeze through the opening at once. They crowded along the rail to point and clap their hands. Some cried.

"Just think, Father," Tran said hopefully. "Our troubles are over. There will be a physician for Sun and enough food to eat. This is Malaysia, our new home."

Father looked thoughtful as he gazed at the dark, irregular line. "It is Malaysia, but not our new home. They don't want either guests or immigrants. However, it is safety. Let's bring up the family." And he slapped Tran on the back.

Amid the commotion and bubbling voices, Tran bundled their meager belongings into the packs. There were sewing articles, a slim copy of the Psalms, writing paper and a pen. Father had kept a diary on ship, and was disappointed when Tran would not.

The pirates wouldn't have found anything valuable here, Tran thought. *We used every kip of our money to buy passage*.

Then he slipped the straps of his own pack over his shoulders. After these few days on ship, the backpack felt strange. If they couldn't stay in Malaysia, would they have to trudge around the world looking for a place to live? Would he feel the pack's cutting edges forever?

Father spread Sun's mat in a corner of the deck, while they impatiently watched the land form into rugged forested mountains, banded by a strip of white beach.

Suddenly Tran heard the engines cut back. "Prepare to let go anchor!" shouted the captain.

Puzzled, Tran watched the scurrying crew. The ship was still a long way from land.

The captain's voice came again from the bridge. "Any farther, and the Malaysian gunboats will fire on us. Two lifeboats are being lowered. I can't spare more. Get in and head for shore. Good fortune to you. You will need it."

At the captain's words, pandemonium broke out on deck. People ran for the lifeboats. "Only two?" someone shrieked. "They won't hold us all!"

Paw began to cry at the noise and confusion. "Shhh, Daughter, we will be all right," soothed Mother. She climbed into a boat, and Father put Paw on her lap and propped Sun against her shoulder. Then Tran and he climbed over the side and wedged themselves in the overcrowded boat.

The two boats sank deeper and deeper under their burden of people, boxes and packs, until the water came nearly to their rims.

"We'll never make it! We'll be drowned!" A voice in

Tran's boat started a chorus of wails and screams that swelled each time a wave lifted them.

A couple of men seized the paddles and tried to push the craft through the giant billows, but there was too much weight, and they gave up to drifting. Waves that had towered and washed over the ship deck in the storm now washed over them. The blinding spray splashed wildly in Tran's face.

They would capsize, and he couldn't swim. Of course, neither could Sun or Paw, and probably not Mother. His face was so wet he couldn't tell if the salt he tasted was from the sea or his own tears. His water-soaked nails turned back from his fingers as he gripped the side. It hurt, but he had to hang on.

The pounding against the boat became fiercer. Were they floating into the breakers? The men had taken up the paddles again and were trying to keep the lifeboat from going broadside. It rocked and pitched, wavered back, then pitched forward once more, until Tran felt a tremendous vibration as the boat grated harshly onto the sand.

A large group of people had come down to the water to watch. As Tran fought to catch his breath, only a few stretched out helping hands.

"I'll take Paw!" He jumped over the side and carried a drenched, whimpering Paw onto the beach.

People screamed and cried hysterically.

"Thank you! Thank you very much!" One man cried that over and over as he put his palms together and repeatedly bowed. Then he sank to his knees and bowed his hands to the earth.

The crowd parted, and Tran was startled to see a group of Malaysian policemen, carrying carbines, approach. What would they do?

The police walked over to the second boat, which had

spilled its passengers and their belongings into the breakers, and stood, hands on hips, waiting to see who would make it to the beach. Tran and Father ran to help their former shipmates.

"Quick! Our grandfather!" someone cried. An old man with a long white beard was tenderly laid on the sand. He moaned softly. Tran looked at the police. Would they help or would the old man die? He wondered if this was the man whose beard he had stumbled over the first night on ship.

"Get an ambulance," said one policeman to another, and then they began to count the refugees. The sun beat down. A long time passed, and still the boat people stood or squatted on the blistering sand. Tran felt too light-headed even to swat the flies that buzzed around him.

He watched the old man's family gently pull a blanket over their grandfather's face.

"He was old and too exhausted," one comforted another. "At least he escaped the Communists."

Tran stared. He felt sick, as he had burying the bodies in the jungle. He had never watched anyone die. Cold shivers ran through him. Death was so final.

More time passed. He was glad when at last they were told to get in a line. It was something to do.

Then a family from the front of the line came back crying.

"The police demand payment," they sobbed. "We had nothing to give them, so we are being sent back."

Tran saw the frightened look on Mother's face. He was frightened too.

Father looked grim. "Maybe they misunderstood," he suggested.

But as the the line progressed, more people came back, some wailing the same story, others saying that they had money, but because they were Chinese, the Malays wouldn't let them stay.

"What will we do?" Mother implored. "We have nothing."

Father shook his head. "Maybe they will take my old wristwatch," he said doubtfully. "But it's cheap, and I don't know if it works after getting wet."

"Why do they not want Chinese?" asked Tran. He couldn't bear to see the terrified faces and hear the crying.

"Because, Son, there are many Chinese here in positions of business. The Malays are afraid new ones will take even more jobs away from them."

Tran thought of Pastor Oh. "But that. . .that. . ." He couldn't find the right words. "But they can't turn them away!" he finally exploded. "They'll be killed if they go back home." Then he realized that could also happen to them if they couldn't pay the police. Terrified, he looked at Father. What could he do? Mother's eyes were closed.

When they reached the front, a uniformed man sat behind a table-barricade. He looked at them sharply. "Name!" he demanded.

"Savang," said Father.

"You do not look Chinese, so you will go to Palau Bidong." He held out his hand. "There is a docking fee, however."

Father took off his watch. The official looked at it and laughed. "That is worth nothing!"

No one said anything.

"No fee? Then get back in your little boat and push off." The policeman waved his hand at them.

"One minute, if you please."

A man who had already passed through came over to them. It was the one who had offended everyone with his *durian* and disagreeable behavior. What did he want?

70

The man bowed to Father. "My actions on the ship were less than kind; yet you were generous and gave food to my family. Would you do me the honor of accepting as repayment a gold necklace?" He offered a beautiful chain to Father.

Tran could hardly believe his ears. That man now doing something kind for them? Tran was a little ashamed for begrudging him the seabird.

Father accepted with many thanks and turned to the policeman. "Will this do for the docking fee?"

The Malay official's hand closed over it swiftly. "This is fine," he said, his eyes glinting with greed. He made a show of stamping a paper and handed it to them. "Next!"

Those who had paid their fee were being herded into the backs of army trucks. As Tran waited to climb into one, he noticed that those who had been turned away were being forced, at gunpoint, into the lifeboats. Would their ship wait for them? He glanced at the spot where the freighter had been. It was already a black dot on the horizon. "*No!*" he cried. "They can't do that to those people!" But in the babble of voices, no one heard him.

With tears streaming down his face, he pushed himself into a truck and sobbed as though his heart would break.

The trucks ground their gears and lumbered slowly away from the beach, leaving behind the lifeboats and the lonely figure covered by a blanket.

Tran stared through the back opening. He said aloud, "That ambulance never came."

11

The inside of the truck was hot, and Tran squirmed as they bumped and bounced along a road filled with potholes. He tried to see where they were going, or at least where they had been, but too many people crowded the opening.

At last they pulled to a stop, and Malaysian police poked and prodded everyone off the trucks in front of a row of matching warehouses. Nearby, a dock, lined with small boats, reached into a bay.

The police herded half the people toward the warehouses. "You stay here until we send you to another camp," they shouted. Tran saw the man who gave them the necklace disappear with his family into one of the buildings.

Then Tran's group was pushed toward the dock, where they were motioned to get into the boats. Each launch filled with people and chugged out to sea.

Where were they going? All Tran could see was the chop of the water. Their destination was Palau something. Father had said that was the Malaysian word for island.

Father and Mother were in front of the boat; so he yelled to the man next to him. "What's the name of the island?"

"Bidong."

"An island might be nice," Tran said eagerly. "Peaceful."

The man looked at Tran and shook his head.

After a couple of hours, a spot of gray appeared on the horizon. It grew larger, and soon Tran saw a small hump of thick forest.

"The island can't be more than one kilometer by one kilometer," said the man sitting by him.

It looks more like one by one centimeter, thought Tran. Where was its beach? Instead of a strip of white sand, the green jungle seemed to come right down to the water.

The eager voices on the boat died down as they approached the island. "Look at that!" someone said.

Tran looked. No wonder he hadn't seen a beach. It was buried under thousands of bamboo and tin shanties, jammed up next to each other. Some were even piled and crammed on top of one another. Their blue-green canvas roofs began at the water's edge and blended into the green rain-forest mountain that made up the center of the island.

From the small dock, a sea of faces looked down into the boats, and hands reached out to lift children, packs and boxes. More blue-helmeted police, also carrying carbines, broke through the crowd and directed the boat people to a makeshift, plastic-walled building.

A metal badge shone from the chest of a big Malay, who sat at a desk and wrote down the names and countries of each family. "Section ten, house number forty-six," he said gruffly to an interpreter, who translated in Laotian. "Curfew at 10:00. Stay in the enclosure, or you'll be shot. Don't talk to the local villagers, or you'll go to jail. Get food at the next desk."

A sign with a large red crescent hung over a table where a lady handed out paper bags.

"Maybe there will be *orlam* or something sweet," Tran said excitedly. He looked at Mother and added quickly, "Of course it won't be as good as yours."

Through an interpreter, the Savangs learned that the United Nations, with the help of the Malaysian Relief Society, would provide food for them once a week. The lady gave them five bags, one for each of them, and said to come back next week for more.

Tran couldn't wait. He peeked inside his sack. There was a packet of uncooked rice, a small flat can with a picture of a fish on it, another small can with a picture of a chicken, a tiny packet of sugar and a lot of tea.

He couldn't believe his eyes. It would make a good dinner, but what were they to do the rest of the week. *Oh,* he thought, *they want us to catch our own fish. That might be fun.*

The heavy rain, plus the feet of thousands of people, had turned what little sand or grass was left into thick squishy mud. It felt cool and good, oozing between Tran's bare toes, as they picked their way around cut-up logs, old tin cans and people. People were everywhere. A solid mass of them sat under the palm trees, which were empty of coconuts. Others milled about aimlessly, jostling each other or clustering in front of huts. Tran couldn't take two steps without bumping into someone. How could there be so many people in the whole world, let alone this tiny island?

"This is house forty-six," Father said, pushing aside a dirty canvas door curtain.

The hut had one small dark room, into which no light came except that which came through the cracks in the walls. It was barely large enough for the five of them to spread out their mats, and was empty except for a wooden box that the former occupants had evidently used as a table. An old fish can with a candle in it sat on the edge. The beach was the floor.

Tran wrinkled his nose. "Whew," he said. "It stinks! Do you think the ones here before dug their bathroom into the floor?"

A knot of people had followed the Savangs to their

home. "Of course. Everyone has to do that," laughed one. "There's no privacy outside for a bathroom. You'll get used to it." The man stopped laughing. "I've been here a year, and I hardly notice the smell."

"A year?" Tran was shocked. A year in this place! "Can't you go somewhere else?"

The man's eyes clouded. "Where? The people in this house before you got to go to America, but I put my application in a long time ago and still don't have a sponsor." He turned and left, followed by the rest of the onlookers.

Tran stared after him, partly because he was thinking about what the man said, and partly because he didn't want to turn back to the dark, smelly hut. "America," he said aloud. He didn't know what the man meant by a sponsor, but he knew he liked how it felt when he said the name, "A-mer-i-ca."

Outside their canvas door, the charred remains of a fire was surrounded by tin cans and other litter. Tran began picking up the garbage while Father went to see if he could find firewood.

"What you do with that?" The question came in broken Laotian from a boy leaning against a neighboring hut.

"Throw it someplace, I guess." Tran felt irritated at such a stupid question. "Wherever we're supposed to throw garbage."

The boy laughed uproariously. "There no place to throw. Malays not want to carry away. Against rules. Leave there. All right."

Tran frowned and scooped everything into a pile. Mother wanted it cleaned up. After awhile he would find a place to put it.

Then he looked curiously at the other boy. He wanted to ask why he talked so funny, but didn't think that would be kind. So he asked, "You are not Laotian, are you?"

"No, Vietnamese. My name, Xuan."

Tran tried to pronounce it, and the boy laughed again. "Say it S-o-o-ng."

Tran tried again, and this time the boy nodded. "I know your name," he said. "I hear your family."

"How do you know Laotian?" Tran asked.

"My family here long time. Other Laotians here, too. I learn. I learn English, too," he said proudly. "I know, 'Hey, man!'"

"What does that mean?" Tran wanted to know.

"That the way Americans say hello. I learn and go to America."

Tran was interested. Here was someone else expressing a wish to go to America. He grew thoughtful. Maybe he should learn to speak English too.

"Hey, man!" he said to Xuan. And then he laughed. It felt good.

When Tran's father came back, he brought with him a bucket of water. "The water in the island cistern is putrid," he said. "So every three days each family is given this much water, brought from the mainland. There won't be enough for washing or even cooking, only drinking."

"How will we cook our rice?" Mother asked.

"We shall have to get water from the sea, and try to boil out the salt." Father gave a wry smile. "But before we can do that, we must sneak into the jungle to bring back firewood. The Malaysians don't supply it."

"What!" gasped Mother. "But they shoot people who go outside."

Father shrugged. "There is no other way."

"May I go too, Father?" asked Tran.

"I don't think it wise for both men of the family to go. I'll try it first."

"Oh, no." Mother had opened two cans of the chicken with the small keys attached to their undersides. "Just look. There's only one small chunk of chicken in each. It's mostly water! And with no fire to cook rice, what will we eat?"

She gave a big sigh and looked so sad, Tran patted her arm. "It's all right, Mother. A couple of spoonfuls of cold chicken broth is all I want. Besides, I may have a taste of sugar to go with it. Give the rest to Father and the girls."

"Tomorrow," said Father, "we'll have firewood, more food ... somehow ... and medication for Sun. It will be better."

"Yes, Father," Tran said listlessly. He couldn't get up his hopes again.

That night, as rain streamed through all the cracks in the hut and Tran buried his face in his mat, one thought gave him comfort. He would learn English and find out all he could about the one place that might be the answer. He fell asleep, saying over and over to himself, A-mer-i-ca.

12

When Tran awakened, he thought he was back on the ship's deck. He was cold and damp, and his muscles were stiff. His hand flopped out and touched the coarse, cold sand beside his mat, and then he remembered where he was.

"I smell smoke." He jumped up and pushed aside the curtain. Father squatted in front of the door, tending a sputtering wood fire, while Mother poured a packet of rice into an empty tin can.

"I'm glad you didn't throw all these away," she said when she saw Tran. "I've washed some out with sand and seawater, and we'll use them for cooking and drinking utensils."

"Xuan said it was against the rules, anyway," said Tran. "They have the strangest rules here." He put another log on the fire. "Like not leaving camp or talking to the local villagers."

"It's from fear," replied Father. "The Malays are afraid we'll take their food and land. They were forced to give us shelter, but they want to get rid of us as fast as possible."

"What if *they* were going to be shot by Communists and had to escape like we did?" Tran said bitterly. "How would they want to be treated?"

"But they haven't been in that position, my son, and so they don't think about that."

Tran scooped back a fly-away ember. "Would Americans send us back to die?" He stared into the flame, thinking of the Chinese and others who had been set adrift in the lifeboats.

"I don't think so, but America isn't like other countries," Father said. "It's made up of refugees like us. They have a history of caring about people." He made a roll out of the rice Mother offered. "Tomorrow morning we must take Sun to the physician."

"I hear there is little medicine, and acupuncture is the only pain relief method," Mother said quietly.

"Yes," agreed Father. "But the talk is, an American physician comes tomorrow. Everyone thinks he will make miracles."

"What do you think, Father?" Tran stuffed some rice in his mouth.

"I think an American physician knows how to help along a miracle."

Tran glanced over at Sun. He hoped Father was right. He swallowed his rice and made a face. "I think after that we should see about going to America," he said. "Rice cooked in seawater is not so good."

The next morning Mother, Father and Sun stood in a long line that stretched from the open side of the tin-roofed medical shed. The physician hadn't come in yet. Tran, who wanted to catch a glimpse of the American, sat nearby in the hot sun and listened to the excited chatter. He amused Paw by rolling a pebble back and forth.

A sudden commotion in the compound made him look up in time to see a tall man in a white uniform striding into the small building. Tran watched the man survey his surroundings with a disgusted look, come back out, and scan the crowd. Tran had never seen anyone with a yellow mustache or so much curly hair, the exact color of sand! The man grinned when he saw Tran gazing at him open-mouthed, and he beckoned.

Tran looked around. Did the physician mean him? Holding Paw's hand, he approached, not knowing what to expect.

The man leaned down. "English?" he asked.

English! What was it Xuan taught him? He thought, and said, "Hey, man!"

The white giant laughed. "Hey, man!" he returned, and reached down and slapped Tran's palm.

Paw's eyes widened, and she watched Tran's face to see if this huge person was hurting her brother. Then she giggled as the man tweaked her nose.

He handed Tran a paper sack, pointed to the hundreds of used paper tissues and other litter on the floor, and said, "Pick up."

Tran guessed what that meant. He had nothing to do; so he took the paper sack and nodded. Helped a little by Paw, who thought it was a fun game, Tran worked, and from the corner of his eye watched the American examine expectant mothers, wounds and crying babies. He seemed to be kind to everyone.

When it was Sun's turn, Tran noticed the physician lifted her gently to the table and stuck two ends of an instrument in his ears. While he talked to her, he put the disc-shaped other end on her chest. Sun gave a wan smile and rasped out a cough. The curly head nodded. Then he put away his instrument and turned to Tran. "Burn the sack," he said, holding out some matches.

Tran understood. He would have liked to have stayed to see what they did to Sun, but now he wasn't worried. With the American physician in charge, she would be all right.

Later Tran scrubbed the wood floor with some strong-smelling liquid, and when he finished the physician, through gestures and pointing at his watch, made Tran understand he was to come back tomorrow. He ruffled Tran's hair and gave him a small coin.

Tran looked at the coin in amazement. Money, just for

having something to do and watching the American! He smiled, bowed his thanks, and ran off to tell his family.

Xuan caught up with him outside. "You get coin?" He looked at it wistfully. "Come, I show you how to buy rice."

He led Tran to a corner of the camp where new mangrove growth obscured the barbed-wire fence. Looking around carefully, he motioned Tran behind the trees. A hole, large enough for a person to climb through, had been cut in the fence. Xuan put his finger to his lips and they knelt, waiting for what, Tran didn't know.

After a few minutes, a rustling of the undergrowth announced the arrival of someone on the other side of the boundary. Xuan hissed something, and the Malay fished around in a large bag and produced a tiny box of rice. He said something back and held out his hand.

"Give him your coin," whispered Xuan.

Tran looked at his pay. He could tell it wasn't worth much, but the number on it indicated it was worth more than this tiny bit of rice. He looked questioningly at Xuan.

"That is the price. Give to him," Xuan ordered.

Obediently, Tran traded. As they made their way to the huts, Xuan explained, "That is called black market. If we go into the local village to buy something, we may be shot. So some villagers come to hole in the fence to do business, and charge much money."

When Tran repeated that information to his family, Father shook his head. "It's too bad—for them, as well as for we who have to pay. Making dishonest money eventually brings grief to one's family."

He turned the tiny box over in his hand. "Thank you, Son. We can use all we can get. Your sister needs rest and nourishing food to go with the physician's medicine."

"Perhaps he'll give me another coin tomorrow," said Tran excitedly.

"Don't count too much on that," cautioned Father. "I understand the American government doesn't pay him to come here. He helps because he is concerned about us, but doesn't have much money himself."

Tran's heart felt as though it would burst. The American physician truly was a good man, and he had singled out Tran to help him!

"I have news too," Father said. "The man with whom I went to the mountains for wood this morning is secretly building a fishing boat. When it is finished, we'll go by night to catch fish."

Mother's eyes grew wide. She started to speak, but turned around to stroke Sun's hair.

Father looked at the back of her head. "If we are careful, he thinks it will be all right. Tomorrow morning Tran will go with me to help." He patted her shoulder. "You will like my other news. The Refugee Committee learned that I was a headmaster, and have asked me to organize a school."

Mother turned around. "A school? Will we be here long enough to need one?"

"I don't know," answered Father. "It is said we must wait until a United Nations representative comes to camp, and then fill out an application for the country to which we wish to go. It may be awhile. But in the meantime," he said, slapping Tran on the back, "we musn't forget what we have learned."

Hours before dawn the next morning, Tran and the two men crept stealthily from camp. Father's flashlight lighted the way into the jungle, where the man pulled a small, crudely made boat from a hiding place. He and Father then gathered sealing pitch to be boiled, while Tran chopped logs with a borrowed axe. After a couple of feverish hours of hard work, they chose their steps carefully back down the mountain before the sun's first rays would reveal them.

Tran flopped down on his mat. He had a sore, where something on the jungle floor had scratched his bare foot, and he was so tired and hungry he wanted to cry.

It was first light now, and Bidong was awakening. Hundreds of wood fires, lit to cook the morning rice, sent their smoky fingers through every crack in the Savang hut. At the same time, a high-pitched din of voices filled the air. Tran slammed his fist into the sand.

The classes Father organized under the palm trees helped Tran's spirits. School gave him something to think about. He had always found mathematics to be fun; so he helped the younger students make a game out of adding and taking away pebbles from a pile. Older children he taught to puzzle out the answer to a problem, using letters instead of numbers. As Sun's health improved, he made up lessons for her. He enjoyed all of this, but what he really looked forward to was each afternoon, when he went to the medical building.

"Why you want be around sick people?" Xuan asked crossly. He wanted Tran to spend the afternoons with him, watching the black-market trading. "You not get much coins."

Tran admitted that part was true. If the physician had extra money, which wasn't often, he gave Tran a coin for burning the refuse and scrubbing the floor. But what Tran couldn't explain to Xuan was that he would do the work free, just for the chance to watch the physician. There was something fascinating about the pattern of first deciding what someone's ailment was, and then selecting the right instrument or medicine for it. There was also something satisfying in the looks of appreciation from the patients. No, he didn't think Xuan would understand; so Tran just shrugged whenever the question came up.

The boat was soon finished and hidden in a little cove. The first time Father went out in it, in the middle of the night, he returned with a large catch of fish for eating and trading on the black market. However, his voice shook when he said to Tran, "I don't think I will go out in it many times. It's so flimsy, each wave nearly breaks it up; and even in the dark, one can tell there are many sharks. Also, the Malaysian gunboat circles the island, and it is difficult to keep out of its way."

Tran shivered. He wished Father would never go again.

It was August now, and one morning as Tran gazed at the graceful fanlike leaves of a palm tree, he suddenly wondered about the flame tree in his back yard in Laos. Had it bloomed, or had it been destroyed like the defoliated trees on the Cambodian shoreline? He hadn't thought of it since he left, and a wave of homesickness swept over him.

It was then he noticed a crowd gathered on the beach. His first thought was of the fishing boat. Had the police found it? He ran down for a closer look. The crowd pointed to a small dilapidated boat, floundering in the surf.

"It rightly flies a distress flag," said a bystander. "It will never make it."

Tran saw an arm wave, and then he stood horrified as a giant swell slammed into the rickety boat, breaking it in half and throwing its passengers into the water. A group of local villagers jeered the boat people as they tried to fight their way ashore amid the floating debris of boxes and wood from the boat.

Tran and several camp people plunged into the water to help those who were too exhausted to wade through the surf. He and one of the victims, a boy, worked together to carry in an old man. Then, as the boy collapsed on the sand, Tran's heart nearly stopped its beat.

"Sy?" he questioned softly. He looked again, and this time he shouted. "Sy! It *is* you!"

The gaunt-faced boy opened his eyes. "Tran," he gasped. "My friend, Tran." Then he closed his eyes again.

Tran looked frantically around for a sign of someone he would recognize from Sy's family. There was no one. With feet that almost flew over the ground, he sped to the medical building. The physician's long legs raced with Tran back to the spot where Sy lay, and he tenderly carried him back to the clinic.

"He needs rest and food," the doctor gestured to Tran after examining Sy.

Tran thought of his family's cramped hut. There barely was room for them, but he knew they wouldn't turn Sy away.

After a few spoonfuls of chicken broth from the Savangs' meager supply, Sy fell asleep on a mat next to Tran's. Tran was impatient for him to wake up. He thought he would explode with all the questions he wanted to ask. What had happened the night the Communists invaded? How did Sy get on that old fishing boat? Where was his family?

But it was several days before Sy was strong enough to do much talking. Besides the fact that his formerly round face was now thin and old-looking, his eyes were clouded with sadness.

"He has had much pain," whispered Father to Tran. "Wait for him to tell us about it."

Sy's story came haltingly. "That day we were dismissed from school. Remember?"

Tran nodded, not taking his eyes from Sy's face.

"Communists marched into town. They ordered us from our homes."

"The shots we heard . . ." Mother said softly.

"They kept us walking day and night. No food. No water. I think it was to kill the weak." His voice broke. "It worked. My grandmother . . . They wouldn't even let us bury her. . . ."

Mother offered Sy some tea, but he shook his head. "We marched inland to the Vietnam border. . . ." His voice had a faraway sound. "Then we worked hard in the fields. . . . We escaped."

"Do you mean, you and your mother and father?" interrupted Tran.

Sy nodded. "We wandered a long time in the bushland. Then some Sky Soldiers found us."

Sky Soldiers! Tran's throat felt tight. He looked down at the dirty string on his wrist.

"They took us to a place where we could get a boat. . . ." Sy's voice broke again.

"What happened?" Tran couldn't contain himself.

Sy began to cry, silently. Then he wiped his eyes. "Patrols check families traveling together. When they shouted for us to stop, we ran. They fired. . . ." He started to cry again. "They killed my mother and my father. I got away to the boat. . . ."

It was quiet in the hut. Tears misted Tran's eyes, and he swallowed hard.

Father laid a hand on Sy's shoulder. "You will be our second son and will go with us when we leave here."

Sy said nothing. He just stared at the ground.

As the days dragged by, the monsoons eased.

"The drier weather is better for you, my daughter," said Mother, as she gave Sun her medicine. "You don't cough so much."

The drier weather also meant less mud to slog through going to school. English classes had started, taught by a Vietnamese teacher, and Tran put his whole heart into the study.

In their first lesson, the teacher pointed to words on a small blackboard and said slowly, "Excuse me, Sir."

Then the students repeated it until each did it correctly.

Aahh, thought Tran. *Just as I supposed. Americans must be very polite people. And this must be how they say hello, instead of Hey, man.* He practiced hard to say it perfectly to the physician.

Sy went with Tran to classes, but didn't seem interested, and many times Tran saw him staring into space.

"Just think," Tran encouraged, "if we go to America, how nice it will be because we have learned the language and kept up our studies."

"But I never liked to study as you did," said Sy. "Remember? I would rather fight with the kites."

"If we study," tried Tran once more, "maybe we can someday go back and help our people."

Sy looked out to sea. "The Sky Soldiers aren't waiting until someday. They fight the Communists and help our people right now."

Tran didn't answer. That same thought had tormented him many times.

On the day the United Nations representative was expected, Bidong awakened earlier than usual and was a flurry of anticipation. School was dismissed and everywhere Tran went, he heard the babble of excited voices.

He met Xuan outside the little post office. "My father tell U.N. we wish go to France. Relative there," said Xuan. "Where you go?"

"America," Tran said proudly.

"Maybe not so good. Many people want go there."

Tran was about to reply, but the sight of several gunboats at anchor in the bay wiped everything else from his mind.

"Father! The U.N. representative is here!" he shouted, dodging every which way in his haste to get back to the hut.

For the next few days, launches filled with refugee families shuttled between the island and the gunboats. Tran's family, with Sy, went out to meet their U.N. representative and be interviewed.

The official pointed to Sy. "Is this also your son, Mr. Savang?"

"No," said Father. "His family was killed, and so he will stay with us."

"Sorry," said the representative. "He will have to fill out his own application for whatever country he desires and wait his turn. He cannot go with you if he is not part of your family."

Tran felt as though a boulder had dropped on him. Of course Sy must go to America with them. Weren't they best friends? Sy had no one else.

Mother patted Sy's arm. "It's all right. You fill out your application for America, and we will wait until you can go."

After filling out their applications, they were taken to another boat where an American immigration officer asked questions in such a loud voice Paw's chin began quivering.

We aren't deaf, thought Tran. *Does he think we'll understand better if he shouts? He isn't like the physician.*

"What skills do you have to offer America?" barked the official.

Father explained that he had been the headmaster of a higher school. The officer then reached for Sy's application, but suddenly Sy pulled it back and tore it in half.

"I will not go to America," he said flatly. "I must go back to Laos!"

Tran caught his breath. Maybe Sy really didn't mean that. But as he looked at his friend, a cold chill settled around his heart.

13

The steady roar of the outboard motor was the only sound Tran heard as they went back to camp. Mother and Father were silent, and Sy just stared ahead, his chin jutting in a determined set.

"*Bon jour,*" whispered Sun when they returned. She sat propped up against the outside of the hut and gave a wan smile at their arrival.

It made Tran feel good these days to see life coming into her once more, and usually he tried to smile and say cheerful things around her. But this time, somehow he couldn't do either. Sun looked from him to Mother and Father, with a pucker between her eyebrows.

Sy squatted beside her and pulled a shell from the pocket of his tattered trousers. "Look, Little Sister. I spied this in the sand as we got off the launch."

Sun caught her breath, and turned the rosy-colored shell over in her hand. Tran knew she was beginning to think of Sy as part of the family. How could they tell her he was going back to Laos?

That night, as the curfew siren sounded at 10:00 Tran was still trying to persuade Sy not to leave. He finally gave up when Sy said, "Don't you see? I have to go back. My father would not let himself believe we could be in danger from outsiders. Because of that, my family died ... and others he could have warned."

He looked intently at Tran to see if Tran understood. "Don't you see?" he repeated. "I have to. I have to make up somehow."

Tran bit his lip. He looked down at his wrist string, remembering the Sky Soldier's story. A big sigh escaped as he nodded and pounded gently on his friend's arm.

Sy left camp almost as abruptly as he had arrived. Now that he had made his decision, he wanted to waste no time.

"I managed to hide a little money from the Communists," he said to the Savangs. "With it, I'll buy boat passage to Thailand and stay around a refugee camp. When Sky Soldiers come for ammunition, I'll go back with them across the border to Laos. Then I will begin my fight." He banged his fist into his palm, looked at Mother, and smiled wryly. "I think they will let me join them, even though I am lowland Laotian and not Hmong."

Until the day Sy left, Father tried to dissuade him. "An American family will surely take you in. You can finish your schooling and perhaps open an import store like your father's."

But Sy only shook his head.

Mother held him close, then looked into his eyes. "You are truly like a second son. That part of me doesn't wish you to go. But I am Hmong. I know there are things that must be done, even when the cost is high. Go in peace, my son."

Tran felt a lump in his throat. He looked at his friend. Somehow, as Sy stood there with bare feet, dusty torn trousers and no shirt, he looked just as much a Sky Soldier as Nao had.

"Sy, we don't believe in the spirits," Tran said as he took a piece of string from his pocket. "But this will mean there is a bond of brotherhood between us that can never be cut." He tied the string around Sy's wrist.

Sy looked solemnly at the string, then touched the one on Tran's wrist. "Yes. Wherever I am, when I look at the string I will remember there is someone who cares about me."

He climbed into the launch that would take him to the ship port and saluted Tran. "Until we meet again, Brother."

Tran waved as the launch started on its way to the Malaysian mainland. He knew they would never meet again. This good-bye meant forever.

When the boat was a small spot on the horizon, Tran went back to the hut. But before he got there, the Laotian saying about the Hmongs being "too tough to cry" collided with his tears.

One hot September afternoon, when Tran finished cleaning the medical room, the physician looked up from his paperwork. "Good job," he said, mopping his forehead.

Tran had learned enough in English classes and from the doctor to understand some of the language when he heard it, but was still unsure of his own ability to speak it properly. So he only bowed and smiled in reply to the compliment.

The physician leaned back in his chair and smiled back. Tapping his pencil on the desk, he said slowly and distinctly, "Tomorrow interviewers from American charitable organizations will be here. Do you understand?"

"Americans . . . here," Tran replied. He didn't know what the two big words meant, but maybe that wasn't important.

"One of them is from the same organization that sent me," the physician went on as he pointed to himself.

"Aahh, yes." Tran caught the meaning of that. Excitement stirred in him.

The curly-haired doctor wrote something on a piece of paper. "Here is the name. Your family . . . go tomorrow." He handed the paper to Tran and gave him a slap on the back.

Tran found Father making school lessons under a small

palm tree that didn't offer much shade. He handed Father the paper and excitedly repeated what the physician told him.

"We will go," said Father. "Perhaps they'll find someone in America who will sponsor us."

Tran couldn't sleep that night in the stuffy hut. Would the interviewer like them enough to recommend them to Americans? Tran thought of his clothes, the same ones he had on the day they left home. They were in tatters. What would the interviewer think? He heard Mother and Father tossing and turning on their mats. Were they worrying too?

The next morning in front of the hut, Tran ran a wet comb through his hair and helped Mother by drawing Paw's hair back and tying it with a length of string. He looked down at his shirt and suddenly remembered—he had another one!

He went inside the hut, opened his pack, and pulled Mother's plate from the center. Making certain no one watched, he unwound the shirt that protected it, until the gleaming black and gold surface was exposed.

"Hurry, Son," came a voice outside.

"Yes, Father," he called.

Tran noticed with satisfaction that the plate wasn't cracked or chipped, and quickly peeling off his ragged shirt he wrapped it securely around the plate and put it carefully back in his pack. Then he pulled on the other white, short-sleeved shirt.

When he emerged from the hut, Mother looked up in surprise. "I didn't know you had another shirt in your pack," she said, puzzled.

"I saved it for something special," Tran quickly answered. He hoped she wouldn't ask more questions. He would surprise her with the plate when they finally were settled.

The interviews were again held aboard gunboats anchored in the bay, and hundreds of people waited to be shuttled out in the launches. After the Savangs stood in line for several hours in the hot sun, Tran's fresh shirt was wet with perspiration. He wished he could take it off while they waited, but Mother said dampness would make big wrinkles in it.

When their turn finally did come, it was no better aboard the boat. The small room to which they were directed was sweltering. In back of the two women interviewers hung a picture of a large statue of a woman holding a torch. Many boats sailed around the statue's base, and underneath the picture, big blue letters spelled out "AMERICA."

One of the interviewers smiled at Tran and his family. Something in her eyes reminded Tran of the physician. What was it? He looked closer. Yes, that same look of caring was there, and kindness. That was it.

"Hi," she said to Tran, and he jumped. He was staring. That was bad manners, and shyness engulfed him.

"Hel-lo," he said in English, slowly to make certain he said it right.

She looked at the piece of paper from the physician. "If Jim recommends you, you must be a special family," she said through an interpreter. "Some of your background information is on your U.N. application, but there is no birth date for Mrs. Savang."

Mother looked embarrassed. "The Hmong did not record those dates," she said. "I don't know when I was born."

"That's all right," the lady said sympathetically. "Many people have that problem. American immigration needs a date, however; so you may choose one, and we will put that down."

Mother thought a minute, then gave a year that she guessed would be close to her age.

"And the month," said the interviewer, showing Mother a calendar.

"Oh, choose the time when the flame trees are in bloom," cried Tran. "You have always liked that."

"Yes," said Mother. She looked at the calendar. "I will take that," she said, pointing to the first day of June.

"Then that is settled. Your new birthday is June first." The lady wrote it down on an application form. "It says here that you have another daughter, Sun, who has tuberculosis." She looked questioningly at them.

"Yes," said Father. "However, she gains strength each day, and the physician says she soon will be well."

"Fine. If we can find someone to sponsor you in America, you will need an official statement that all your family is free from disease." She looked at Mother and Father and said hesitantly, "I hope you will not mind my curiosity as to a Hmong and a lowland Laotian being married. I understand usually the two hardly speak to each other. And you're both Christians, not Buddhists or Animists."

Father told, through the interpreter, how Mother's family revered education, and had made enough money selling the opium flower to send their daughter to Vientiane, to a school which he also attended. The two fell in love and wanted to marry.

Tran wished Sun were there because she always liked hearing that part.

Here Mother broke into the story. Tran was surprised, because Mother never mentioned the story to anyone.

"My family . . . they were very angry," said Mother, shaking her head. "They told me not to come home if I marry a lowlander." Her voice broke. "But how could I not?" She gazed at Father, then lowered her glance.

The interviewer listened as Father told about Pastor

Oh, and how they had decided that for them the God about whom he spoke was best, even though it meant persecution from family, friends and many townspeople.

Tears glistened in the young woman's eyes as she stood up. "We will send your background information to churches, schools and other organizations in America," she said, shaking hands with Father and Mother. "I can't promise you when you will hear that someone will sponsor you, but I hope it is soon. Jim was right to recommend you. You *are* special people."

The following week, Sun had a happy smile when she returned from a checkup. "Brother! The physician says that even though I need more medicine and rest, I can no longer give the lung disease to anyone; so we can go to America. *C'est merveilleux!*"

"Yes, it indeed is wonderful!" agreed Tran, putting both arms around his sister.

He was happy for her and for them, but he felt each hot, draggy minute of the next few weeks. Every day he went to the community bulletin board to check the list of names of those who had received sponsors. And every day he shuffled back to Mother and Father with the same story. The Savang name wasn't on the list.

"America is a big country," consoled Father. "It takes a long time to communicate to all the organizations our interviewer told us about. We must be patient."

That was the hard part for Tran. He wanted to be free from the barbed-wire prison. The desire to race across his town's grassy hill, with Blue Star sailing above, overwhelmed him, and one day he tried to fashion a kite from sticks and pieces of brown paper bags. But it wasn't satisfactory, and with hordes of people everywhere there was no place to launch it.

He begged to go to the mountain every morning for the firewood, just to have a few moments of feeling alone. The jungle smelled cool and damp. Water caught in huge, pitcher-shaped flowers tasted warm but good, and a giant bamboo tree, when slashed, spurted out water that was cooler than that brought to the camp from the mainland.

As a little morning light squeezed between the dense trees, Tran was often startled by a demoniacal shriek that split the stillness. Once, when Xuan was with him, he explained to Tran that it was a hornbill, a large, weird bird that patrols the elevations.

How free it is, thought Tran, as he watched the black shadow move across the jungle roof. It can go over the barbed wire, even over the other side of the mountain, if it wants. He wondered if it could fly across the ocean. That thought was so intriguing it found its way into his dreams, where he had gigantic black wings and soared over the large statue that stood in the American harbor.

More than once, though, his dreams turned into a nightmare, as he looked down and discovered his wings were made of sticks and brown paper, and then he would crash into a sea of barbed wire. He always awakened from these bad dreams with a pounding heart, and the feeling of terror would remain with him all day, especially as he watched other families who had been in Bidong a shorter time than they, packing to leave.

"Some people high up on list," explained Xuan knowingly. "They officers in army, so they picked first. Others, one, two in family, easy find place to stay." He sighed. "Six in my family. Not so easy."

There are five in our family, thought Tran. *That won't be so easy, either.*

Since Mother had implored Father not to go out in the

fishing boat again, their food consisted of the meager packets they lined up to get once a week. Sun's appetite was returning, and Tran tried to share his food with her, but he was so hungry. Father had long ago sold his watch on the black market for a little rice and dried fish, and a few times that Tran was in the jungle he found roots to cook. Once he uncovered some large black beetles that he stuffed in a cloth sack and took home for Mother to roast.

"This isn't so bad," he said in a surprised tone, after gingerly biting into one. "It tastes a little like nuts."

It took too many beetles, however, to make even a small meal; so he gave up trying to collect them.

Xuan announced one day that his family had caught a monkey.

"How did it taste?" Tran asked curiously.

"Strong and sweet," answered Xuan. "I not like it all time, but . . ." He shrugged. "It helps us stay alive."

There were only two important things in the world anymore, it seemed to Tran: staying alive, and seeing your family's name on the bulletin board. And the weeks dragged slowly on, centered around those two things.

Then one day, toward the end of October, as Tran finished burning the hospital refuse, the physician came up to him and clapped him on the back. "Congratulations, Tran!"

Tran looked at him, puzzled.

"Do you mean you haven't . . ." began the physician. Giving Tran a slight push, he directed him to the bulletin board and pointed.

Tran looked, looked back at the doctor, and looked at the list again. There it was! SAVANG. . . . .FAMILY OF FIVE.

Tran let out a whoop, dashed away, ran back to bow to the laughing physician, then rushed away again, to shout to a thousand huts that the Savangs were going to America!

14

As Tran raced to find his parents, others, hearing his shouts and anxious to know details, joined him, until a huge crowd finally stopped at Tran's hut.

"You are going to America!" someone shouted to the Savangs before Tran got the words out of his mouth.

"When do you go?" asked someone else.

"Where in America are you going?" asked another.

"I don't know," said Father. "I had better find out these things."

Amid much laughter and back-slapping, one woman called, "And this means a new skirt for Mother!"

Tran looked at Mother's ankle-length skirt. It was ragged and stained, and she did like pretty clothes. If only . .
While Father went to the administration office, Tran sat in deep thought.

When Father returned, he was excited. "We leave in a few days," he said. "As soon as our official release papers are made out, we take a launch to the mainland and a bus to a transit center camp."

"Transit center camp? What is that? Aren't we going to America?" Tran asked in a disappointed voice.

"Yes, Son, we are," Father said. "But we must stay in a transit center for a while so more medical examinations can be made, and also our flight arrangements."

Tran was bewildered. "Flight? Not a ship?"

"No," said Father. "We will be on an airplane. There is much to be thankful for. Even though we still don't know who or where our sponsor is, we will be free again."

The family joined hands in a thanksgiving prayer, but inside Tran was a tumult of feelings. An airplane flight and being free again were wonderful things. But he would have to say good-bye to Xuan and the physician. And Mother needed a new dress for the journey.

Later, as Father sat alone by the cold ashes of the campfire, Tran asked him about an idea he had considered.

"No, Son. I do not want you to go out in the fishing boat. It's too dangerous." Father looked stern.

"But, Father . . ." Tran felt a little frightened. He had never argued with Father before. "The man who built the boat goes out all the time, and nothing happens. It'll be all right. I can sell the fish and buy Mother some material. She needs some new clothes," he finished, as he saw Father start to shake his head.

Father stared into the dead embers. After a few moments, he said, "If it were not for the fact that your mother does need something new, I wouldn't allow you to go. And perhaps I shouldn't anyway, but . . ." He looked at Tran. "You are careful, and you have proven yourself a man. For your mother's sake, you may go."

Tran wasted no time in dashing off to find the boat's owner, and in the middle of the night the two crouched in the darkness, waiting for the armed guard to pass their spot.

The sound of heavy steps came toward them. Could the guard tell they were there? Tran held his breath. Now it seemed the sentry had stopped. But no, the steps plodded on by, through the deep sand.

Tran silently exhaled and crept with his partner to a clump of thick shrubbery. His heart pounded against his ribs. All the guard had to do was unexpectedly retrace his path, and they would be caught!

They dragged the small craft over the sand several

inches at a time, stopping to listen. Tran cringed when he heard the water slap the wooden sides. Anyone close by could hear that too.

"Get in," the man ordered in a hoarse whisper, and Tran obeyed. He felt the shaky skiff sliding into the water, and silently the man got aboard and began to paddle into the inky blackness.

They put down the fishing lines, but the little boat was being tossed around in the waves like a feather, and it was hard to hold onto the line and the boat at the same time.

It was just as Tran caught his second fish that a strong wave lifted them into the air. Before he could think, Tran was catapulted through space. A scream tore from his throat, then died as smothery water closed over his head.

The next instant he broke the surface of the water, took a big gulp of air, and thrashed his arms around. His right arm hit something. It was wood, maybe a piece of the boat. He pulled himself to it and threw his other arm over it. "Help!" he screamed.

In the darkness, he heard more sounds of thrashing, then the other man's voice. "Tran!"

"I'm here," he called back. "I'm holding onto something."

"I am too. Hang on." The man's voice rose and fell with the waves. Then he yelled, "Aahh! Get away from me! Sharks! Stay as still as you can!"

Tran froze. Sharks! He felt something bump his leg. A shark? He tried to hold still.

"Get away from me!" he heard the man yell. "Help!"

At that moment, a light out of the blackness shone on Tran, and he heard men's voices and splashing water.

"Pull the boy aboard! Get back, you sea-devil! Get the other one!"

100

Strong hands pulled Tran up, and he landed face down in the bottom of a boat. After that, he heard no more until Father's voice, from a long way off, commanded, "Lay him on the mat."

Tran roused from the fog to feel someone tearing his trouser leg.

"Oh, no!" He knew that was Mother's voice, and he looked down to see what bothered her so much. Blood streamed from a gash in his leg.

As Mother bathed the wound, Father said, "I am so sorry, Son. I never should have allowed you to go." He covered his eyes with his hand.

Tran couldn't clearly see Mother's face in the flickering candlelight, but heard her whisper, "Why?"

"You needed . . . a new dress," Tran managed between groans. He felt pain as Mother's fingers probed the wound.

He took a few deep breaths, then gasped, "Got two fish. Could have caught more . . . sold . . . for material." He closed his eyes and fell asleep as Mother tied a bandage around his leg.

Not long after dawn, Sun came in the hut, followed by the physician, who bent his head as he entered. After blinking his eyes in the dimness, he went to Tran, who propped a blood-soaked and bandaged leg on a mound of sand.

Without a word, the doctor peeled away the bandage, treated the wound, then bound it again with clean bandages. "Couldn't you think of another kind of bait to use for fishing besides yourself?" he joked to Tran.

When Tran understood, he tried to smile. "Yes," he said in halting English, through flinches of pain. "But I wanted another chance to watch you work."

"With all the observing you have done at the clinic, you could have taken care of this," said the doctor as he closed his bag and stood up.

Tran didn't know what "observing" meant, but he understood the rest. He grinned widely and nodded.

After the physician left, though, gloom settled over Tran. He wouldn't be able to walk for many days. Thanks to him, their departure would be delayed and maybe the United States would think they didn't want to come. He should have listened to Father.

Filled with despair, he didn't realize Xuan had come in the hut until the younger boy sat down beside him. "I heard about shark," he said, his brown eyes wide. "Authorities hear too, but they not know who."

He looked at Tran in admiration. "You brave to stay still. Some story to tell."

"The story will be that I kept my family from going to America because I couldn't walk," said Tran, bitterly.

Xuan jumped up. "I must go," he announced, retreating in haste.

Tran sighed. *No one will stay when they learn of the disgrace I've brought my family.*

The next morning he gingerly tried putting weight on his foot, but it hurt too much. He groaned. *There is no way I can get to the transit center,* he thought. *Father can't carry me.*

Just then, bright sunshine flooded the hut as Xuan entered. "Here something help get you to America," he said, proudly thrusting something at Tran.

It was a long stick, carved from teak wood. Tran ran his hand over its smoothness. He stood up and balanced himself on one leg. The stick was wide and rounded at the top and just fit under his arm. He put his weight on it and started to hop around the room.

"Look! I can walk with this! Where did you get it?"

"Last night in jungle. Then I work on it until now," replied Xuan in a pleased voice.

"Many thanks, my friend," exulted Tran. "The physician said something about walking sticks, but they had to come from the mainland and would take a long time."

He practiced walking some more. Around and around the hut he clumped. It was hard to keep the end of the stick steady on the sand while he hopped on the other foot. The area under his arm hurt, but he made himself keep going until he could do it smoothly.

"Thank you, thank you," he repeated. "Oh, I wish you could go to America too, Xuan. Then we could see each other sometimes."

Xuan looked down and drew a circle in the sand with his toe. "No. My father no wish. He say Americans not so kind to foreigners. We try go France."

Tran stared at him. Xuan's father was wrong. He knew it. Americans were good and generous and kind.

Many friends came to the launch to see them off.

"Write a letter, please," Xuan beseeched.

"I will," promised Tran. "And may you be sponsored soon."

The physician broke through the crowd with a big smile on his face. "I see you are all healthy enough to enter the United States."

Father bowed deeply. "Thank you, Doctor, for all your kindnesses." It came out partially in English and partially in Laotian, but the physician understood and shook hands with Father and Mother.

He put his arm around Tran's shoulders. "Do not give up on your talent. Someday you will make a fine doctor."

Tran fought down a lump in his throat as he swung his leg over the side of the small boat. How many more good-byes would there be—good-byes that meant forever?

"Farewell," he yelled as the launch roared away. He

waved until he could no longer clearly see the dock. "Farewell, Palau Bidong," he murmured, watching the island turn into a hump of green.

Was it his imagination, or did he hear a demoniacal shriek coming from the forested crown of the island? Someplace up there a giant black shadow flew across the jungle. Perhaps it was angry that he had escaped. Tran shuddered and turned toward the mainland.

Hours later, their dust-covered bus rolled along paved streets crowded with people. Father sat across the aisle from Sun and Tran.

"You are now in the largest city in Malaysia," he told them.

"Oh," cried Sun. "Look at the lights. Red, green, yellow, and . . . They're everywhere. What are they?"

"Those are neon lights," explained Father. "They are signs for the markets."

"And look at the buildings," said Tran in awe. He tilted his head to try to see out the bus window. "They are so tall. Where do they stop?"

"They are bigger than those in our town," laughed Father.

Their happy mood fled quickly, however, when the transit center's gates loomed in front of the bus.

"We are in prison again," said Sun as the gates closed behind them.

"But only for a short time, my daughter," Father reassured.

"What . . ." began Tran. But he decided not to ask the question he had wondered. What if their sponsors changed their mind about taking them? Where would they go?

Inside, the camp reminded Tran of Bidong. People crowded together like ants. As he stepped from the bus, the same noise and confusion hit his senses.

There were some differences, though. As the new arrivals from Bidong lined up to have their papers stamped and to receive food packets, he noticed that the people behind the desks were not Malays, but were of many different skin and hair colors. One, with curly, light hair, reminded him of his physician. Each wore a name tag with U.S. at the top.

"A floor," Mother said appreciatively as they entered the room assigned to their family. Tran gingerly slid his foot across the splintery wood. It was better than sand. The room was about the same size as the one at Bidong and was in a row with ten others, just like it, all under the same roof.

"Do you want to look around the camp?" he asked Sun.

She readily agreed, and the two went off to investigate. They discovered that there were outside communal bathrooms with attached showers. "That will be nice," Tran said, remembering that Bidong had nothing.

"Look," said Sun, pointing to a line of people at a water faucet. "At least we can get water when we need it. Mother will be glad."

Just then the people in line seemed to melt away. "Water pressure off," grumbled a man who passed Tran and Sun. "There never seems to be water before the evening meal."

Tran's leg began to hurt; so he and Sun returned to their room.

"The camp might have a few things better than Bidong," said Tran, "but it has the same feeling."

For several days they lived as they had on Bidong, except wood was provided for fires, and there was a store, selling food and merchandise to the few who had money or something to trade.

Father immediately volunteered to help in the camp school, "because," he told Tran, "if one works, the mind is occupied and time seems to go faster."

The time going faster appealed to Tran, and he offered to help tutor the young children, as he had on Bidong, even though he got around slowly on his crutch.

One day a notice was placed on the community bulletin board about upcoming Christmas activities; so he also volunteered to plan children's games. He thought there would be only a few in camp who would celebrate Christmas, and was amazed to learn that nearly everyone, even those who were not Christians, anticipated the holiday.

"What can I do for so many children?" he asked Sun in dismay.

She considered a moment, then went to her pack and pulled from it an object wrapped in brown paper. Carefully unwrapping it, she held up a stick figure, dressed in regal clothes and wearing a gold crown. "My shadow puppet," she announced. "I thought I was bad to bring her along, when we were supposed to bring only important things. Except," she added softly, "my puppet was important to me."

Tran smiled and shook his head at the feelings of girls, then quickly sobered as he remembered the Blue Star. He would have brought it with him, if it had fit in his pack.

"Sister," he said gently, "would you help me entertain the children by organizing a shadow puppet play?"

"That is what I thought," she said smiling. She gathered together boys and girls of all ages and, in spite of the fact that they all spoke different languages, helped them fashion other puppets from pieces of plastic, paper sacks and sticks, to present in a Christmas play she wrote with Tran's help.

It took a week to decorate the camp. They used shredded garbage bags, so the trees would look like pine trees; garlic and onion ornaments; cotton for snow (Tran didn't know what that was supposed to look like, but the American teacher said it was necessary); and every kind of paper for paper chains. Even the adults participated in the volleyball, Ping-Pong and Chinese chess tournaments.

The American workers brought in apples, candy and small wrapped presents. By the twenty-seventh of December, Tran and everyone in camp was exhausted. But for those few days, they forgot they didn't belong anywhere.

The American in charge of the camp's education program heard about Tran's fishing experience, and one day he and another teacher brought Mother a bundle, neatly tied with string. With a puzzled look, Mother unwrapped the package, then caught her breath and softly said, "Oooh" as she held up several lengths of rich, black silk.

At first she couldn't believe it was for her, but when she understood she said simply, "Thank you. Now I shall not disgrace my family when we arrive in America."

Tran hadn't seen such a pleased look on her face for a long time, and while he wished he had been able to present the material to her, the important thing was that she had it.

"I have seen women from other countries wearing pants instead of a long skirt," she said. "That's what I shall make." And for two days, she spent nearly every daylight minute bending over her work, until she had made not only a pair of long trousers for herself, but one for Sun and one for Paw. "Now we are ready for a journey," she said, stroking the silky fabric with satisfaction.

Late one afternoon, the first week of January, word was sent for them to pack and be ready for processing before boarding the airplane. They had little to pack, but Tran and Sun wanted to say good-bye to new friends. So Tran scarcely had time to feel excited until ten o'clock that night, when they stood outside the administration office with a hundred other refugees. He noticed how nice Mother and his sisters looked in their new clothes, and as they were given a plastic bag with the number 17 in bright blue crayon, anticipation of the journey began to well in him. In a few minutes, they would board a real jet!

His anticipation soured, though, as the few minutes stretched into hours. They were counted, checked, marched, bused to the airport, counted again, then checked again.

"I want to sleep too," wailed Sun, looking at Paw, contentedly curled in an airport chair.

"Try not to, Daughter," said Mother. "They may call us any minute to get on the airplane."

But they didn't get called. Hours went by, and dawn arrived.

"I'm hungry," grumbled Tran under his breath.

Mother heard him. "They will surely give us something to eat after such a long wait," she soothed.

But breakfast didn't appear—only other passengers, checking in for the early morning flight, who made Tran uncomfortable with their stares at his walking stick. Some even gestured to each other about the scar on his face. Tran had nearly forgotten about it, but now he was self-conscious.

Just before noon, they were marched out to a huge blue and white jet that said CLIPPER AMERICAN on the side. Tired and hungry though he was, that sight made Tran's heart skip a beat.

When they were belted into the seats, Sun yawned. "It's like a bus."

Tran looked around. How could this enormous thing with so many people on it possibly fly? As the airplane thundered down the runway and lifted into the air, panic hit him, and he gripped the arms of the seat. He finally loosened his deathlike grip when a uniformed lady reached across him, pulled down a tray, and put a plate of food on it. "Lunch?" she asked with a smile.

108

Tran smiled back. The food looked so good and there was so much. It was more than he had seen since home. There was chicken and rice, juicy pineapple chunks, and a sweet cake!

He kept his chopsticks busy and ate ravenously, until the sweet cake. Then, partly because he wasn't so hungry anymore and partly because he wanted to savor every bite, he made the cake last until he heard the pilot explain over the loudspeaker that they were approaching Hong Kong.

Father gazed out the window in awe at the China hills in the distance. "That was the home of some of our ancestors," he said to the family.

Tran, sleepy and filled with food, was too drowsy to respond and in a minute was in a sound sleep, disturbed only when they landed in Korea.

As they headed across the Pacific Ocean, on the last lap of their journey, the air became bumpy. Soon sick groans came from all parts of the airplane. Tran felt sick too. He tried to fight the feeling, but gave up to the embarrassment of using the airsick bag. When he felt a little better, he thought, *I wonder if the hornbill gets airsick?*

A few hours later, a cry went up. "America!" And everyone left seats and went to one side of the airplane to try to catch a first glimpse of their new home.

"We will soon be arriving in Seattle," announced the flight attendant.

"Not San Francisco?" asked a woman disappointedly. "I thought it would be San Francisco. I have heard of that."

"No," replied the attendant, "but Seattle is nice."

"See-attl." Tran tried out the name. It didn't sound quite the way the attendant said it. He looked at Sun. "See-attl," they both said together, then laughed.

With so many crowded in the aisle, Tran couldn't see

anything outside; but when they were told to go back to their seats, he stretched and peered out. They were high above a blur of green. A jungle?

Out of the green, a large cone, a mountain of frosty white, reached toward them. Ooohs and aaahs went up from the passengers.

"That is Mount Rainier," said the uniformed lady as she walked down the aisle.

"Mount . . ." Tran gave up on the last word.

Soon the plane dropped lower. "Look!" called someone. "Now there are buildings as far as you can see."

The airplane banked at such an angle Tran couldn't see. Was Seattle like Bidong?

He felt as though he were going to slide out of his seat, and his body strained against his seat belt as the big jet touched down, then screeched its wheels on the runway. With a noise like a dragon blowing out hot breath, it slowed and shuddered to a stop. People began crowding the aisle again, anxious to leave.

Tran sat still. They had made it! They were free! But as he looked at the acres of concrete and strange buildings surrounding them, he suddenly felt afraid.

What would they find when they stepped from the airplane? What kind of world and life was ahead?

15

As everyone filed out of the airplane door, a man directed them down a ramp into a roped-off area. A large sign overhead announced: U.S. IMMIGRATION. Tran clutched the bag that bore their special number and looked around to see if their sponsors waited for them. But all he saw were uniformed people inspecting refugees' documents.

"Every paper you have has your name in a different order," said a lady behind a desk. "Is Savang your first or last name?"

Father, not understanding, shook his head. An interpreter was called, who explained to the immigration officer, "He says his last name is Savang. It's the custom in Laos to put the family name first."

The officer corrected the mistake, stamped their papers, and pointed them to another area where packs were being opened and searched for contraband. Tran swung his pack onto the table, and immediately thought of the plate. Mother would see it!

Quickly he said the first thing that came to his mind. "Mother, does Paw need to go to the bathroom?"

Paw set up a howl. "Paw no have to go bathroom."

By the time Mother decided if that were true or not, the inspection of Tran's pack was finished. He breathed a sigh of relief.

The man in the health department stamped each of the documents, but looked up when he came to Sun's. "Hey, wait. This says you have an active case of tuberculosis. We can't allow you into the country!"

Tran couldn't understand what the man said, and Father looked bewildered. There was a problem, but what was it? Finally, another interpreter was called, who explained to the Savangs what the inspector had said.

"No," said Father, aghast. "She has been under medical treatment for many months, and the physician said she was well enough to come. Doesn't it say that on the document?" he implored the interpreter.

Tran felt as though the world had just stopped. Sun couldn't be denied entrance. Not after they had come this far. He stared at the man behind the desk. Maybe if he stared hard enough, the man would change his mind.

The official's forefinger jabbed at the paper in front of him. "Aren't you Chou La from Vietnam?" he accused Sun.

"This is our daughter!" cried Father. "Who is Chou La?"

The inspector looked again at the paper and muttered something.

"He says," the interpreter explained, "that he was given the wrong paper, and that he is sorry."

Father bowed, indicating he accepted the apology. Tran's knees felt weak. What else would happen?

Others around them, who were going to places called Montana and Ohio, were sent to other parts of the huge airport, to await another flight. Tran decided he liked the sound of O-hi-o, and was wondering if it were a city or maybe an island when he spied a tall man with spectacles, holding up a card on which was printed 17. Next to him stood a little girl about Paw's age, and a slender woman with short dark hair, who looked anxiously at each newcomer who passed.

"Look, Father!" Tran pointed and, not knowing what else to do, held up their corresponding number.

112

A big grin broke across the man's face when he saw the blue 17 hoisted into the air, and he immediately came forward, followed by his family. "Savang?" he questioned, holding out his hand.

Father smiled, bowed, then shook hands.

"We. . .are. . .your. . .spon. . .sors," the man said slowly. "We. . .are. . .the. . .Johnsons."

"Johns-sons," carefully repeated Father, and he bowed again. Tran, Mother and Sun all bowed politely. Paw peeked at the little girl from the folds of Mother's trousers.

"Please come." The man picked up Mother's pack.

Tran couldn't understand that. Mother could carry her pack. But he hitched his own over his shoulders and followed everyone into what looked like a tiny windowless room. Johnson stepped in last and just stood, smiling at them.

What are we do. . . But Tran's puzzled thought was interrupted. The doors snapped shut, and suddenly he felt himself dropping. It was a terrible sensation, especially in his stomach. Sun squealed, but before anyone could say anything the room jolted to a stop and the doors opened.

"All right," their sponsor said, ushering them out. Tran looked around at the people and baggage carts. They were still in the airport, but in a different place. The little room had brought them here like magic. He looked back to see other people inside the room, and the doors closing. He wished he could try it again. The sensation wasn't that bad. Now that it was over, it had been fun.

"Son." Father's louder than usual voice caught his attention. They all had gone ahead and were waiting for him. Tran's cheeks burned with embarrassment as he caught up to them.

They walked by a door through which a blend of delicious smells came, making Tran hungry. A window revealed people sitting on chairs at small tables, eating a meal. They weren't standing or sitting on mats as he was accustomed. How strange.

"Excuse me, Sir." He was so busy looking in the window he had bumped into a man, who looked at him curiously and hurried on his way. Everyone walked in a hurry. Even those who stared and pointed to his family did so while rushing by.

Where were they all going so fast? Oh, to those stairs over there. Tran stopped. Those steps moved! He poked Sun. "Look!"

Both watched in astonishment as people glided onto the steps and were carried almost to the ceiling. Tran turned at a touch on his arm. It was Father, also watching in fascination.

"It is truly amazing," he said. "But come, our sponsors wait for us."

Tran followed Father, but with so many backward glances at the moving steps that he didn't realize large glass doors had silently parted for them and they were outside until the texture under his bare feet became cold and rough, and a chill, damp wind bit through his thin clothing.

He looked down. He was walking on an American sidewalk! And the gray sky overhead . . . it was an American sky! They were here! They were really here!

Mr. Johnson opened the door to what looked like a small bus. "You all may sit here," he said carefully, pointing to a couple of rows of benchlike seats in the back.

Tran and his shivering family gratefully climbed in and huddled together. The sponsor started the motor and pulled away from the curb. In a minute, a flow of warm air caressed Tran's cold feet. Where was it coming from?

The lady sat in front with her husband and daughter and took from her bag a small book, with *Yao-English* on the

114

cover. She turned around and pointed to it, then to Tran's family with a questioning look.

"Aaah, yes," said Father, in halting English. "Laos . . . speak Yao and Hmong." With the last, he pointed to Mother, who smiled broadly at the mention of her ancestry.

"We speak Y—" began Father, but the word was snatched from his mouth as with a roar they left the road they had been on and joined a mammoth one with hundreds of stampeding cars.

Tran didn't know which direction to look. The bus hurtled between other cars, buses and trucks. It was good everyone was going the same way, but it took his breath away. Sometimes their bus would veer in front of another car, catching the family off balance. Mother's face was pale as she held tightly to Paw and clutched Father's arm for steadiness.

Tran was relieved when the bus left the big highway and turned down a quiet street with just a few cars going slowly. Didn't anyone ride bicycles? *How wealthy Americans must be, with so many cars,* thought Tran.

He relaxed and gave his attention to the houses they were passing. There were all sizes and shapes. Each had a patch of grass in front, and most had green shrubs. Tran drank in the peacefulness. It was almost like home.

They stopped in front of a brown house. The Johnsons got out and beckoned Tran's family, which struggled out of the bus. Tran didn't notice much about the house. He was too busy studying the green tree that grew in the center of the yard. It was shaped like a graceful pyramid, and he could hardly bend his neck back far enough to see the top. The leaves weren't leaves. They were soft, blunt needles. He had never seen a tree like it.

"Son," Father called.

Tran turned away from the tree. They were waiting for him again! He made hasty steps to join them at the door of the house, and as they walked in he looked in disbelief. Neither had he seen anything like the inside of this house!

Ahead of him, he saw Mother's foot sink into the thick rug. She stopped and took off her thongs.

"No, it's all right," said the lady, gesturing Mother to put them back on. Mother looked at the lady's shoe-clad feet and nodded.

Tran gazed in wonder at the big chairs and the tables with tall lamps on them. Small logs lay inside a brick opening in a wall. A large table at one end of the room held plates, cups and saucers, and reminded him he was hungry.

"Please ... sit down," invited the lady, indicating a long padded bench. Then she disappeared into another room, and returned a few minutes later, carrying a steaming teapot and a plate of sliced meats.

"Come, eat," she said, motioning them to sit in the chairs surrounding the table.

Sun hesitated, but Tran, remembering the airport restaurant, sat down.

The man bowed his head. "Thank you" was the only thing Tran understood, but that was all right. Their sponsors said a prayer before they ate. It made him feel more at home.

He and his family picked up their meat slices with their fingers as usual, but Tran watched the Johnsons cut theirs and spear the pieces on a metal tool by the plate. Wouldn't they pierce their tongues? Perhaps he would try using that tool sometime.

After the meal, the Johnsons took them down some steps to a large room. A table with a net in the middle was pushed against one wall, and darts in a round board hung on another wall. A large raised platform, covered with cloth, occupied

116

the center of the room, and against the other walls smaller raised platforms were also draped with cloth.

"Your family sleep on those," the man gestured.

"Yes, yes," Father returned enthusiastically. He bowed. "Thank you."

The woman looked around and shook her head. "Small room," she said apologetically.

Tran knew the word *small*. He thought of their rooms at Bidong and the transit center, and smiled. To show them that their family would be comfortable, he picked up his mat and unrolled it on top of one of the smaller platforms.

"When you wish to try the American way," the lady said with a smile, "it is like this." And she pulled away the cloth on top and lay down between two more large white coverings.

Tran thought it looked hot and uncomfortable, but if Americans slept like that, he would try. Besides, he could always put his mat on the floor if it was too bad.

Just then, Paw began to wriggle and whispered something to Mother. Mrs. Johnson understood at once.

"Bathroom," she said, pointing down the hall.

Oh no, thought Tran. Not in the house, like Palau Bidong! Of course he couldn't expect them to have a bathroom like the airplane had, but he hoped for at least a nice outdoor one as they had had in Laos, or even the transit camp.

The sponsors must have noticed his dismay, for they motioned everyone to follow them. As the family all crowded into the bathroom, the sponsors demonstrated how to push the handle down on the oval white object in the middle of the room. Each one got a try at making it work. Then the man showed them how to operate the shower.

By this time, Paw was jumping up and down and pulling on Mother's sleeve. Everyone laughed and, leaving Mother to help Paw, filed upstairs. Mrs. Johnson gave both Father and Tran a small Yao-English dictionary.

"We are glad to have your family," she said, using sign language to help.

"We . . ." Father started to respond, but then he stopped. For as Mother and Paw came into the room, the Johnsons' little girl went to Paw.

"Here," she said, thrusting at Paw what looked like a large puppet, except it was rounded and soft and—even Tran was fascinated—it had real hair, black, tied with ribbons.

"My doll," said the little girl.

Paw looked at this thing in her arms in wide-eyed amazement. Then a big smile broke over her face as she stroked the silky hair.

Father thumbed through his dictionary. "We . . . grateful," he said, tears brimming in his eyes. "We grateful."

That night, as Tran lay between the bed covers, he thought of the night they fled their home. He thought of the helicopter fire and the dead bodies, the Communist soldiers trying to catch Paw on their bayonets, the pirates, the barbed wire, and the shark. He reflected too on how carefully God had protected them.

He lay still a long time, thinking. Then he reached quietly into his pack for his knife, and after hesitating a moment cut the string around his wrist.

He would always keep the dirty, frayed string. It would be a symbol of what they had been through, and what his country and his friends were still enduring. But the purpose for which Nao had intended it was complete. They were safe.

The next few days were a whirlwind to Tran. There were so many places to go and so many things to learn. The day after their arrival, the Johnsons said that shoes are needed in cold weather; so the lady drove them to a store where they could buy a pair. The fact that a lady would be able to drive that small bus amazed Tran. He couldn't imagine Mother doing that.

The sponsor bought thick coverings, called stockings, for their feet, then chose shoes for Tran that she said other boys wore. They were soft white with a blue stripe. But even though Tran thought them beautiful, his feet protested at being prisoner for the first time since he lost his sandals.

Sun didn't seem to mind having her feet confined as much as Tran. All the way home, she looked at her shoes, which were nearly identical to his. And she walked very carefully, so as not to get them scuffed.

The next day they bought heavy pants for Father and Tran, and warm jackets for everyone. Sun got a red skirt.

Father was overcome with emotion. "We cannot repay you now," he said in broken English to the sponsors, "but someday you will be repaid for your kindness."

Television was like something from another world, and Tran and Sun watched it constantly when they were in the house. It was puzzling, however. Did all Americans get so excited about a cup of tea, or the soap they used for bathing? He had never seen gunfights or wild car chases when their sponsors drove them around town. Tran was confused.

One day he and Sun went to the school Mrs. Johnson said he would attend and took examinations. The teacher seemed surprised as he looked over their papers.

"Good," he said, tapping Tran's mathematics test. "You will do well." He said it slowly enough for Tran to understand. Then he spoke rapidly to Mrs. Johnson.

"He says," she relayed to Tran, "that you will begin tomorrow. You will go one half-day here at your school, and Sun will go one half-day at hers. Then you both will go to an English class."

Tran grinned. He was excited about beginning school, and the crinkles at the corners of Sun's eyes said she was too.

The next morning Tran and Sun were so excited, they could swallow only a few bites of rice, though both had been eating eggs cooked in a large pan with slim pieces of pork, the way the sponsors did. Sun spent a long time brushing her hair, and Tran worried he might have a bit of dirt on his clothes that had escaped notice.

After Mrs. Johnson dropped him off at his school, telling him to go to the office and wishing him luck, she drove away with Sun. Tran walked with a pounding heart to the school door. He had sounded out part of the name, carved on a sign in front. Ever-green Jun-i-or H... The last word was hard.

"Hey!" someone called.

Tran turned. Was someone speaking to him? A boy leaning against a tree watched him. Tran smiled. It would be nice to have a friend his first day in school.

"Hello," he said.

"Cripes, the gook speaks!" the boy called to others nearby. "Hey, everybody, say hello to the gook!"

16

Tran took a couple of steps, intending to shake hands, but stopped when he saw other students, who had been lounging against the school building, come toward him. He was surrounded by faces that weren't friendly.

"Look at that scar," someone shouted.

Tran didn't understand, but they were all peering at his face. He put his hand up to his cheek.

"Man, the gook must have gotten that in some knife fight!"

"Probably over a dog. They eat 'em."

A girl made a vomiting sound. "You eat dogs?" she asked incredulously.

"Sure, they do," answered the boy who still leaned against the tree. "Gooks eat all kinds of scum. The other guy must've had one big knife to slit his head like that."

Tran looked from one hostile face to another. He could understand few words, but the students' tone indicated they were angry.

He tried to turn to go into the building, but the group moved in closer.

"All right, break it up!" A voice stabbed into the tight circle.

"Alberts!" someone said, and the group parted as a big, dark-skinned man shoved his way in.

"You've all got better things to do than stand around." The man jerked his head in the direction of the school building, then pointed to the boy leaning against the tree. "Especially you, Kramer."

The boy muttered something, and several girls laughed. The cluster melted away.

"Are you the boy from Laos?" the man Tran decided was a teacher asked him.

Tran nodded.

"I'm Mr. Alberts," the man said. "George Alberts."

Tran started to bow, caught himself, and shook hands instead. "My ... name ... is ... Tran Savang," he said carefully.

The teacher escorted Tran into the school. But when they passed the smoldering eyes of the boy and some of his friends, a knot of apprehension formed in Tran. Why didn't they like him?

The hall was jammed with students, laughing, screaming, talking. It was like Palau Bidong.

He forgot about the morning incident when he learned his first class would be mathematics, his favorite subject.

"This is algebra," the teacher explained, showing Tran a textbook. "Can you do this?" he questioned slowly, with a dubious look.

Tran examined the book, smiled and nodded. Although the instructions were in English, these were all problems he had learned to do the year before. He sat at an empty desk and glanced out of the corners of his eyes at the students. Curious stares from classmates fixed on him the rest of the hour, but Tran didn't mind, as he concentrated on solving the equations.

An hour later, after getting directions from the algebra teacher, he walked through the door of the next class. A high-pitched whine from an electric saw whipped his eardrums. Electric drills hummed, and another kind of saw added its buzz to the din.

Sawdust clung to Tran's new shoes as he crossed the room to show his admittance paper to the apron-clad teacher.

"Welcome to wood shop," the teacher shouted in his ear. He held a block of wood in a clamp; so Tran decided against trying to shake hands, and merely gave a short courteous bow of greeting.

As he went to a vacant spot at a table, he noticed the same boy who had been angry with him that morning, sanding down a piece of wood. When Tran passed him, the boy bowed deeply. Tran started to smile, but suddenly found himself sprawling in the sawdust.

He picked himself up and brushed the wood-shavings from his clothes. Had the student deliberately tripped him? That would be the behavior of a small child. The boy mouthed something and bent over double in an exaggerated laugh, then, as the shop teacher approached, turned his back and vigorously sanded his wood; but his shoulders continued to jerk with suppressed laughter.

A heavy feeling grew in the pit of Tran's stomach, and while he studied the sheet of saw diagrams the teacher gave him, he searched his mind for what he could possibly have done to offend that boy. Had he committed some mistake or oversight in custom this morning? In some unknown way, he must have done something insulting.

After awhile the machines quieted, and the class quickly dispersed, ignoring the teacher's admonition to "clean up your place."

Tran understood the teacher, but as he hadn't done any wood-working, he left, looking back at the messy room. With ears still ringing from the noise, he looked uncertainly up and down the crowded hall, wondering where to go next.

"Hi." A girl with hair that reminded Tran of a sunshiny morning tapped him lightly on the arm. "Do you need help?"

Tran nodded and held out his class schedule. She studied it. "You have P.E.," she said. "Come on, I'll take you to the boys' gym."

As Tran followed her, she tried to make herself heard over the bedlam around them. "Where are you from?"

Tran shook his head, so she tried again. "What country?"

Tran smiled. "Laos."

This time the girl shook her head. "Here's the gym," she said, pointing to two big doors. "My name is Lori."

Tran didn't have time to introduce himself or shake hands or bow or anything, for a loud bell rang and the girl waved and hurried away.

That certainly was one of the big differences in America, Tran mused, pushing open the double doors. Everyone here was in a hurry.

The large room was empty except for a man in heavy gray pants and top. He wore a whistle around his neck, and as Tran approached he recognized the man as the teacher who was in the schoolyard that morning. The teacher looked up and smiled.

"Hello, Tran."

Just then a door burst open and thirty yelling boys, dressing in white shorts and tops, spilled onto the shiny gym floor.

Mr. Alberts blew his whistle. "Quiet down, men!" he shouted, and as the hubbub ceased he put his arm around Tran's shoulders. "This is Tran Savang from Laos."

"Hey, Tran," said one of the boys with a wave of a hand. Tran smiled and tried to wave the same way, but his smile faded at the sight of someone making sing-songy sounds and doing the formal bow, hands pressed together. It was his tormentor. A couple of boys laughed. Tran felt sick.

"Cut it, Kramer," snapped Mr. Alberts. He turned to Tran and gave him a piece of paper. "Give this to your sponsor," he said. "It is about P.E. clothes."

124

Tran sat on a bench and watched the boys bounce and throw a round ball to each other. Sometimes one would toss it toward a net basket mounted high on the wall. It looked like a good game, and he hoped he could soon get clothes like theirs, so he could join.

When the whistle blew and the boys left the floor, Mr. Alberts came over to Tran. "I'll take you to the cafeteria," he said, propelling Tran out in the hall.

Tran had no idea where they were going, but as the spicy smells of food trailed their way toward him, he realized he was hungry. The huge room where Mr. Johnson took him exploded with students and noise.

"Hi, again." It was the girl who had helped him before. La-ree. She had some other girls with her.

"Do you know Tran?" asked Mr. Alberts.

"We just met a while ago," Lori answered. "Tran, will you sit with us?"

Tran looked at Mr. Alberts, puzzled. He understood her question, but should he do it?

Mr. Alberts gave him a gentle push. "Lori will take care of you."

Lori showed Tran a red ticket. "Do you have one like this?"

Tran nodded and pulled one the principal had given him from his pocket.

"Okay," she said, and motioned him to follow her to a line of students.

The other girls giggled. Tran felt strange being in the middle of these girls, but at least they were friendly. "Okay," he responded, feeling almost happy for the first time that day.

With Lori's help, he picked out a round, brown roll that had meat inside.

"This is a hamburger," she explained, and went on to pour mustard and red sauce inside the roll.

Tran did the same on his and bit down. The texture of the meat was different, but pleasing. It was good.

"Where did you say you were from?" Lori asked. "What country?"

Tran picked up a thin slice of potato that crunched between his fingers. "Laos. Then . . . camp."

Lori's eyebrows puckered. "I don't know where Laos is," she admitted.

One of the other girls spoke up. "My parents send me to camp in the summer. No fun, is it?" She tried again and shook her head in sympathy. "Camp . . . not good."

Tran looked at her. He didn't understand what all she had said, but finally agreed with a smile. "No, not good."

A big yellow bus came by for Tran after lunch. It already was filled with other refugee students, some older than he, some younger. No one was talking. As he made his way to a seat, someone tugged at his sleeve. It was Sun.

"Sit with me, Brother," she implored.

He eased into the seat beside her and asked quietly in Yao, "How was your morning?"

"Confusing," she whispered back. "I don't know English as well as you, and I couldn't understand anything."

"You will learn, Little Sister, and then things will go better. Don't worry." But even as he spoke, Tran couldn't help but wonder if things really would get better for either of them.

However, now he would sit back and enjoy the comparative silence as the bus rolled its way to their English classes. After the morning's noise, he was ready for peace and quiet.

"What kind of day did you have?" Father asked anxiously when Tran and Sun returned home that afternoon.

Tran searched for something that would be truthful but not burden Father with worries about him. He finally borrowed Sun's word. "It was confusing," he said. "But tomorrow will be better."

He told Father and Mother about Mr. Alberts, his classes, his new friend La-ree, and the afternoon orientation school where they would learn more English and how to shop in America. He didn't say anything about his problems.

"Aaah, it's good you have a friend. That will ease your confusing days." Father clapped Tran on the back. "And do you know? I will take classes in English in the evenings. And our good sponsor helped me get employment during the day."

"Employment!" Tran was excited. "Are you headmaster of a school?"

"No," replied Father. "I will wash dishes in a restaurant."

Wash dishes. Tran couldn't believe what he was hearing. His father! Besides, Tran didn't think his father even knew how to do that. Tran had been assigned to scrub the galley pot on the ship.

"We are very thankful your father has employment," said Mother, looking sharply at Tran. "Mrs. Johnson says that not all Americans have it."

"Oh," said Tran. He felt ashamed. If employment was so scarce, Father was indeed lucky to have found this job.

The evening meal was a red meat sauce, served over long slender noodles. The sponsors called it "spagti," or something like that.

They provided chopsticks for the Savangs, but this time Tran decided to use the fork. He watched closely as Mr. Johnson wound the noodles around the pronged metal, then put it neatly in his mouth. Tran gave it a try, but the noodles kept slipping off the fork. Finally he decided he didn't care if the noodles did dangle, and he opened his mouth wide and shoved the fork in. "Owww!"

The Johnsons and Mother and Father pretended they hadn't seen his mistake, but Sun and the little girls squeaked with laughter. Tran lay down his fork. He would fight with it tomorrow. The chopsticks allowed him to enjoy the good "spagti," and after his active day he didn't need much urging to have a second helping.

"I learned some English today," Sun announced proudly to Mother and Father.

"Say it for the sponsors," suggested Father.

Everyone stopped eating to listen. Sun sat up very straight in her chair and took a deep breath. "She sells seashells by the seashore!" she recited carefully.

"What does it mean?" Tran asked.

"I don't know," Sun replied. "But our teacher of English made us say it over and over."

The Johnsons couldn't explain what it meant. "It is famous," they said.

Later Tran looked up the word *famous* in his dictionary and shook his head. That must be the famous saying of a great American philosopher. It sounded funny, but perhaps he had better learn it too. Maybe someday he would understand the meaning.

For the next few days, the sameness in routine stirred memories in Tran of life in Laos. It wasn't only because he enjoyed algebra and his other Evergreen school classes, but there was something satisfying about the pattern of a school day.

In wood shop, he leafed through a book showing pictures of projects students could make. When he saw one of a decorative wall shelf, he went no farther, and began working with a happy feeling in his heart. The shelf would be perfect for Mother's plate.

He tried to stay out of Kramer's way as much as possible and never again walked past him in wood shop. It wasn't that Tran was afraid of him, but until he learned enough English to be able to communicate with him and find out what he had done to cause the problem, it was wiser to avoid him. With the shop teacher watching, Kramer couldn't be obvious in his persecution.

The P.E. locker room was the only time Tran couldn't evade him. Some of the other boys tried to be nice to Tran when they would see him in the halls, but around Kramer they changed. When he started taunting Tran, they followed his lead.

Neighbors of the sponsors had given Tran an old pair of shorts, and the first time he changed in the locker room, a howl went up from Kramer.

"Scar-face! You sure are cut up! Bet another gook did that to you with a broken bottle!"

The rest of the boys crowded around, eyeing the long scar on Tran's leg.

Tran wished he had his dictionary so he could explain. What was the English word he needed? "Fish," he finally said, pointing to his leg.

The boys hooted. "Did an itty-bitty fish get the gook?" shouted one.

"Nah," sneered Kramer. "He's just not as good with his judo and his knife as the other gooks." Kramer circled Tran. "He's not a very good fighter." He spit at Tran.

The spit landed at Tran's feet, and Tran's eyes narrowed. The other boys backed up.

"Fight! Fight! Watch it, Kramer, he's probably got his knife on him!"

129

As Tran looked at Kramer, he suddenly thought of Sy. Sy was in a real life and death fight for his country. And here he, Tran, was ready to fight a classmate, just because he spit at him. Those were children's actions.

He dropped his hands from their clenched position and walked into the gym, amid jeers from the other boys.

Sometimes Lori and the girls ate lunch with him; but if not, he hurried through a lonely lunch hour or skipped it altogether. After not having enough to eat for so long, he now felt he sometimes had too much, and he didn't want to waste the food when he wasn't completely hungry.

One day, as he sat with Lori, he was startled by something whizzing past his ear. Then something else sailed through the air.

"Duck!" cried Lori, but it was too late. Splat. Something hit Tran on the forehead. It was a piece of meat. Soon the air was filled with bits and chunks of food. What was happening?

"It's okay, Tran," Lori consoled, using a napkin to wipe red sauce from her hair. "They aren't throwing things at you. Some kids do this all the time. It's called a food fight."

"They . . . play with . . . the food?" Tran looked at the piece of meat that had hit him and remembered the thin, wasted bodies of the people on the ship. He remembered trying to catch the seabirds and the tiny packets of food in camp. What this small piece of meat would have meant! Unable to keep back the tears, he jumped up and ran out of the cafeteria in a hail of food.

That evening when he got home, Mother and Father greeted him with, "The Johnsons found us a house!"

Mother's eyes sparkled, and Tran tried to lift his dragging spirits so he could be happy with her. "That is good news, Mother. But how can we pay for it?"

"The United States government will help pay some of the rent. However, we don't wish to be a burden on anyone," said Father.

"But with the money from your father's employment and from mine, we can pay it ourselves," Mother said with an emphatic nod.

"*Your* employment?" Tran was aghast. Mother employed?

"Our sponsor showed the silk trousers I made to her friends, and they liked them and would like me to sew for them," Mother returned proudly. "And we can move into the house next week," she finished.

Sun came in and the news was repeated to her. "That's nice," she said sadly, and burst into tears.

With much coaxing, the cause of her sadness tumbled out.

"The girls at school said I speak strangely and don't know how to eat properly. They laughed at me." And she dissolved again in sobs.

Father put his arm around her and sighed. "They don't know us or anything about us, Daughter. People are fearful and distrustful of ones they don't know. It will be difficult for you to be kind when they aren't; but if you are, soon they will learn."

Sun dried her eyes, and Tran went down to their sleeping room. Xuan's father had been right. Americans didn't like foreigners, and what was more, Tran didn't think he *ever* would fit into their way of living.

The house looked enormous to Tran and his family, after living in one room for so long. The front porch opened onto the sidewalk, and the tiny back yard was a jumble of tall grass and weeds. Thorny vines entwined a scrawny, leafless tree, and rusty cans and soda bottles lay everywhere. There were no window coverings and no furniture inside the four small rooms, but Mother was happy.

"It is good I have gone with father to English class," she said to Tran. "Now I can say 'hel-lo' to the neighbors."

They probably won't say hello back, thought Tran bitterly. His thoughts were lately more and more that way, each time Sun came home in tears, or he heard another hurting remark by one of his classmates. His English was so good now that he could understand nearly everything that was said, even though he had difficulty speaking.

The day Tran's scarred leg was badly kicked in the P.E. basketball game, Mr. Alberts talked to him after class.

"That was done on purpose, Tran, and I have suspended the boy from class."

"No good . . ." Tran burst out. "Another one . . . and another one . . . I do not belong here."

Mr. Alberts looked at Tran for a long time. Then he asked softly, "What color am I?"

Tran looked up, surprised, and tried to think of the word.

"I am black, Tran," supplied the teacher. "I did not belong here either. Black people were brought here. And Kramer . . . you know where he's from? His grandparents came from Europe. They didn't belong here, originally." Mr. Alberts leaned back in his chair and laughed. "There is a saying that is very wise."

Tran looked at him curiously. Would it be the one about seashells? He waited while the teacher wrote something, then read the piece of paper Mr. Alberts handed him. "Bloom where you are planted."

Mr. Alberts continued, "Tran, many, by a lot of hard work and patience, have done that. You can too."

Tran bowed and walked out of the gym. He respected Mr. Alberts's proverb, but if the soil was rocky, and if the plant was all the time cold, as he had been since coming to Seattle, then it could not grow and bloom.

That afternoon, helping Mother go up and down the strange aisles of the huge food store close to the sponsors' house, he saw some bananas. They reminded him of the leaves they had used in the jungle for plates and to cover the dead bodies. That's where he ought to be, in the jungles, helping Sy and doing something for Laos!

He brooded over that idea the rest of the evening, and it was the first thing he thought of the next morning. Algebra class was a blur, and he seemed all thumbs with his wood project. When Mr. Alberts stood up and talked to the P.E. class about experimenting with an international sport for the next few weeks, Tran wasn't really listening.

"Wow." The boy sitting next to Tran nudged him in the ribs.

Tran jerked to attention.

"And those of you who want to get in on spring baseball may do so after school," Mr. Alberts was saying. "Otherwise, we will compete against Green Lake Junior High in a late-spring kite fight."

A whistle of appreciation went up from most of the boys. "Cool!" said the boy beside Tran.

Mr. Alberts locked Tran's gaze to his. "Tran, have you done that before?"

Tran was flustered. "Fight with . . . the kites? . . . Yes."

"Then we need your ability. It'll be a lot of work. Will you help us?" The teacher's gaze didn't waver.

"Y..yes," stammered Tran.

"Cripes!" he heard someone mutter.

17

The days picked up speed. Besides his studies, it was Tran's responsibility to get the outside of their house livable. Father worked long hours in the restaurant, and went to English and American orientation classes each night with Mother.

Tran borrowed a sickle from their sponsors and cut down the high grass, then started on the wild blackberry vines. One day, when the Johnsons brought over an old stove someone had given away, they also brought summer flower seeds and a small evergreen tree. They planted the tree next to the scrawny one.

"That tree looks dead," said Mr. Johnson. "I don't think it's native to this area, and our cold winter probably killed it. If you can get an axe, Tran, chop it down and toss it."

Tran thought he certainly would cut it down as soon as he could. It seemed out of place beside the graceful evergreen and the broad-foliaged shrubs. *There isn't a tree or flower here that is familiar,* he thought, and a deep wave of homesickness swept over him.

It helped to talk to Mr. Alberts about the kites and materials required for them. When Tran said they needed bamboo for frames, they both made a trip to a large store that sold everything in the world. At least, it seemed that way to Tran.

"There!" Mr. Alberts said triumphantly. "Will that do?"

Window shades, made of split bamboo, hung from a display. Tran marveled. One shade would make at least fifteen kites. Then they shopped for rice paper, lots of glue, and different paint colors. The bright reds, sky blues and clear yellows gleamed from their glass containers.

At school, Tran demonstrated to the P.E. class that making an upward angle to the kite would catch air particles in its pocket and keep the kite level, even when doing aerobatic maneuvers. They didn't even need a tail, except for decoration. Then he showed them how they could make their frames into various shapes. Some chose hexagons, some chose birds or airplanes. Tran made his into a star.

He was surprised that Kramer had decided to enter the competition, and even more surprised at the hard work and care Kramer lavished on his kite, a red hawk. But Tran wasn't about to instigate trouble by saying anything to him.

One afternoon Sun came home with a smile that reminded Tran of their old days.

"What do you think?" She exploded through the door of their house. "Today the teacher read a little about Laos, and then explained about shadow puppets."

"Oh," responded Mother with a fond smile, as she sewed a rip in a chair a neighbor had given them.

"And she said that we would have a shadow puppet play, and would I please help with it!" Sun was so excited she couldn't stand still. "And do you know what else? We began French last week, and the girl who sits next to me asked me to come to her home to help her. *C'est merveilleux!*"

Tran felt so elated for his younger sister that he hugged her. "That is *merveilleux!*"

The kites were nearly finished. Someone who lived near the water brought sand, which would be spread over about 100 feet of flying line, on top of glue. That would provide an abrasive surface that would saw through another person's string. It also was a defense against one's own line being sawed.

"Remember," Mr. Alberts told the class the day they were going to try them out, "in real competition you may keep any kites you cut. In this practice run we won't do that, but you will probably all go home with cut strings and maybe a damaged kite. It takes experience to learn to maneuver properly, and you will all have to learn the hard way."

The class took their kites outside. A light breeze brushed Tran's face and flowed on across the grounds. Newly unfurled tree leaves rustled, and it almost seemed to Tran as if he were on the hill above his Laotian town.

The boys offered their kites to the wind, which plucked at them, then carried them away from outstretched fingertips. Tran began to pay out his flying line in steady motions, taking a few steps backwards, to help keep it taut.

In a few seconds, his new Blue Star had gained altitude and seemed to fly itself in an upper layer of wind. He held it in place and watched the others around him. One boy had let his line out too fast, and his kite landed on another boy's head.

"Mr. Alberts!" shouted someone. "What's wrong with my kite? It won't rise, and the tail just hangs down like an old dog's!"

"What do you think, Tran?" Mr. Alberts called.

Tran bit his lip. This was funny, but it wouldn't do to laugh. So after he controlled his face, he called back, "Tail is too long."

"Thanks, Tran," said the boy, reeling in his kite to fix the offending streamer.

Several flyers, including Kramer, had gained altitude, but their kites insisted on darting around in wide circles. Tran noted with approval that Kramer soon figured out he was flying too flat to the wind and remedied the situation. The others, after thrashing in the air, crashed to earth. Now

136

there wasn't anyone left with whom to compete, except for Kramer and his red hawk.

"I'm going to cut your stinkin' kite to pieces, gook," said Kramer as he moved closer to Tran.

All at once the hurts and bitterness of the last few months surged through Tran like a thunderclap. He said nothing to Kramer, but he could feel his mouth setting in a hard line, and his eyes became narrow slits as he turned his attention to the red hawk. The most important thing in the world now was to disable it, to smash it!

They went through dives, loops and side-to-side runs, and twice Kramer tried to cross Tran's line, but didn't succeed. The other boys, watching at one end of the field, alternately cheered and hooted.

Then, with a swift movement of his wrist, Tran maneuvered his Blue Star into a fighting position. He let out a victory cry as he felt his string meet the rough surface of the hawk's line.

Kramer jerked hard to try to escape, but Tran stayed with him. Then, from out of nowhere, Father's words to Sun echoed in his ears. "If you are kind to them, soon they will learn."

No! Tran thought. *Kramer has made life miserable. He needs to be taught a lesson, to be punished.* His arm moved back and forth in a sawing motion.

All at once, Pastor Oh's gentle face appeared in his mind. He had offered his life—and probably gave it—for his tormentors. With a change of position and another swift movement of his arm, Tran lassoed the hawk and brought it in, dangling from his own line.

A cheer went up from the onlookers.

"Hey, Kramer, he gave you a break!" shouted someone.

Kramer glowered. "Why didn't you cut it?" he demanded. "You could have."

"I almost did, but chose not to," Tran answered quietly. "You have a beautiful kite. You will be a fierce fighter."

Kramer shrugged and disentangled his kite from Tran's. "It was dumb!" he insisted, his face flushed. "Bein' nice doesn't pay."

It was Tran's turn to shrug. He labored over the right English words. "That . . . depends on who your . . . employer is," he said.

"Aw, I don't even know what you're talkin' about," growled Kramer, winding up his string. He gave a false-sounding laugh to the boys who were approaching with Mr. Alberts. "The gook was too chicken to cut my line!"

Mr. Alberts stood with his feet wide apart and his hands on his hips as he gazed steadily at Kramer. "I happen to know a little about Tran's story," he said. "I don't think that some-one who rescued his sister from being bayoneted and got slashed by a shark would be too chicken to cut your kite string. There must be another reason. Why don't you ask him sometime?"

The boys, including Kramer, all stared open-mouthed at Tran.

"Yeah, well, maybe . . ." mumbled Kramer, picking up his kite and walking alone back to the school building.

The rest of the boys surrounded Tran, slapping him on the back.

"Gee, Tran, did you really do all of that?"

"How come you didn't tell us?"

"Say, do you want to come over tonight and help me fix my kite?"

Tran, astonished at this sudden shift in attitude, turned the corner. With a big grin he looked from one face to another. Maybe conditions would be better.

He caught a glimpse of Kramer's lonely figure opening

the school door. Perhaps conditions would change there, too. Kramer would probably never be a friend, but Tran had a feeling that a truce had been called.

Mother's new birthday, June 1st, came a few weeks after the Savangs had been in their house. Tran finished the shelf and proudly presented it to her on that peaceful Sunday.

"You did this?" she exclaimed. "It's so beautiful. It looks like work your father has done," and she closed her eyes, picturing, Tran guessed, the teak table and other furniture of their old home.

He secured the shelf to the wall, then went to his old pack, which was under his bed. When he returned, he carried his old tattered, blood-stained shirt, which he slowly unwound. Mother looked at him inquiringly.

She gasped as the shiny black bordered plate with the gold design was revealed; and as Tran put it on the shelf, she breathed in loudly. Tran turned to look at her face. Was she pleased?

Mother stared at the plate and ran her finger lightly over the smooth rim. Then, and Tran thought he would never forget this as long as he lived, her eyes filled with tears that fell unheeded down her cheeks.

After a moment, when Tran wondered what she was thinking, she put her arms around him. "Thank you, Son," she murmured. "Thank you." And her flowing tears wet his face.

A sweet fragrance, floating on a cloud of softness, had permeated the air. It beckoned one outdoors, but Tran had been so busy with end of school studies, he hadn't had time to pay attention to their yard.

One morning, as he pushed aside the curtains, his heart did a somersault. The ugly, scrawny tree was covered with reddish gold blooms!

He raced outside and tenderly examined the branches and blossoms. They . . . they were like the ones in Laos. It was a flame tree! Not the same tree he had been used to. Some of the time it was very different. But in the end, it was the same. He couldn't explain it, but that was satisfying to him.

He stood back and gazed at it. "Tree," he said softly, "you and I are the same. We are from another place."

He sighed, shook his head, and thought, *We were planted in soil we don't understand.* He reverently touched a blossom. *But you survived . . . and maybe I will, too.*

With his heart ready to burst with emotion, Tran pressed his hands together in a deep bow.

"We will bloom," he whispered, "where we have been planted."